BRUTAL DREAMS

JD Cowan

For my friends and family, past, present, and future. Special thanks to my readers and fellow writers. May the Lord always smile down upon you.

BRUTAL DREAMS

Local Community Report

On July 13th, 20XX, at approximately 1:30am, three civilians reported a loud explosion in the woods. Similar reports of scattered gunfire from deep in the trees followed. Voices were heard in the night air. Investigations uncovered nothing out of the ordinary.

No further noise disturbances reported. Investigators believe it an elaborate prank.

CHAPTER I
Lost in the Fog

Death pressed against his lungs, waking Christopher Archer from his deep slumber. Red air slipped through his tightly shut eyes, presenting a world of crimson fog shrouded in night. Cold and heat burned under his skin. He felt around to find he was in his car, upside down and in the driver's seat. He unbuckled and his weight slammed against the ceiling. How did he get there? His memory was a scramble of static, missing patches like an old passed down family blanket, and everything ached as if he fell on a pile of broken glass. The crash had really done a number on him.

Archer clawed at the car window, hoping for escape. He wrapped his shaking fingers on the lock, fumbling it open. His breaths wheezed and crushed in on his lungs as the fresh air poured in from outside. It tasted like rotten eggs.

He tumbled out of the car and struck the grass, a deeper shade of red momentarily knocking him senseless. The rouge fog coating the night sky didn't help.

Waves of sickness slithered up his stomach. His knees trembled under him with every attempt to rise. The world twirled and bent around his flickering sight. Finally he forced himself up.

The car engine gave no response. Once, twice, and three attempts, led to nothing at all.

How did he even get here to begin with? His brain buzzed at his attempts to think. He remembered leaving home for a meeting at the mansion in these very woods. The last memory he had was of driving down the forest road and seeing some sort of shooting star in the sky . . .

Archer grumbled and rubbed his sore skull. Now he would be late for his appointment.

He checked his phone and swore. No power. The young man would have to find help for himself.

Visibility was getting worse by the minute, and that stink of rot was setting in. There was no other way to go on this lonely forest road than forward and hope he could find the turnoff on his own. The mansion had to be close. There he could get his bearings straight again. Archer abandoned his overturned car for the pavement of the road, hoping some passerby might see him. His feet carried him forward as if they had a mind of their own.

Archer's steps echoed in the dead silence of the forest. Wind whistled through the high trees. Those tall branches blocked the view to the sky, including any moonlight. If it wasn't for the red glow of the surrounding mist he wouldn't be able to see anything.

"Ariane," he said, involuntarily. He had just seen her, hadn't he?

"*Stop!*"

Archer looked over his shoulder and no longer saw the road. He now stood in a dark room where a red-haired woman was being held by a man in a black suit. The young woman screamed, but no one appeared to hear her. On the floor lay a giant of a man, wearing the same suit, spitting copious amounts of blood from his mouth. He twitched around like a corpse.

An old geezer in a blue suit with nicely polished shoes kicked the downed behemoth. He glanced at the red-haired woman with a sad smile.

"*This is what happens when you run.*"

Jolts sparked through Archer's brain, and his knees nearly buckled. A small, sphere-shaped baseball of pain spun in his grey matter. Memories and pictures he knew, and some he didn't, rocketed through his mind.

When Archer finally looked up, the dream had ended, but one thing remained. He knew that woman. It was her: Ariane. His fiancé. She was alive!

Archer hurried forward, desperately searching for the path he needed. Eventually, he found a simple dirt road that winded up into a slope hidden by trees and red fog. This was it!

He pulled up the collar on his grey trench coat and scanned the silent forest. Cold wind like death clung to his bones, and he could swear it sounded like someone speaking to him in the breeze. The only sounds were his shoes scuffing the dirt carpet of a trail. He never heard as much as an owl's hoot. It was like walking through ruins of a bombed out forest from some old war. Archer kept his mind on the Beretta in his coat even if his thoughts kept circling back on Ariane. She was the reason he was here, after all. And she might be alive!

Her father had called him to this place, and Archer would oblige his request. He had no remaining business with this old man he had never met before. In fact, Archer should have stayed away from these woods. Perhaps he still had a nostalgia lingering for the old times torn from his empty insides which drew him here. It was about the only feeling he had left in his rotting soul beyond a vague hatred for everything. Archer was told to come alone, and he did. But he couldn't help but wonder. What kind of a father steals his daughter from her fiancé, especially a father that wanted nothing to do with her before now?

Even in his darkest moments, Archer thought of Ariane. He remembered those familiar dimples on her neck and those supple lips, as well as the thin and soft fingers when he held them tight in his in cold weather. Her golden-red hair shone like holy light in the blackest of nights. Those better times were eons ago, even though it had only been months in reality. When he reached McKinney's mansion, he would learn the truth.

Humidity clung to Archer's skin like dirty thoughts in an old-time burlesque show. He ran a pale hand over his sweat-covered crew cut and pounded his old bowler hat free of a leaf and small twigs. Did the wind suddenly stop?

"*I see you.*"

Archer spun on his heel and went for the Beretta. No one waited behind him but the quiet of the night. The silence deafened worse than a bad rock concert, leading him to scan the trees with his sidearm outstretched. McKinney might have sent someone out here for him, but he couldn't stop the young man. Archer would not leave without *her*.

At the edge of the nearby brush, a figure fogged into existence in his peripheral vision. The stranger had brown crew cut hair, Caucasian skin, an eagle-like face, and a familiar grey trench coat. It was Archer! This person could be his twin! The doppelganger contained his broad shoulders and bowler hat, as well as the long coat, but there were no defining features on the face under the hat brim. Only shadows moved where the eyes should be.

"Who are you?" he asked the stranger.

The slamming of wet meat slapping against a butcher's counter was all the sound it made. One couldn't even be certain it was making that noise from its mouth. Hard breaths soon pumped from its non-moving chest.

This thing wasn't human.

Archer's nerves seized, leaving him unable to think. The creature didn't budge, it did not even breathe despite the sound. Archer struggled to keep his own breathing steady as he willed his legs to move backwards from this monster.

A voice cast itself high above the trees. "*I see you.*"

Archer drew his Beretta. The barrel couldn't even glint from the lack of moonlight, yet the weapon felt like a beacon of light in the hard fog. The figure did not shrink at his threat.

"I asked who you were, friend," Archer asked.

The sidearm clicked, but the ghoul did not move.

Instead, it disappeared. The creature faded like a mirage into the night air as if it was never there to begin with. Archer quickly found himself alone on the shoulder of the road again.

Brush shuffled behind him. A large purple creature emerged from the dark, looming down with a hand outstretched like a pointed hook. Unlike the doppelganger, this facsimile of a person wore no clothes on its featureless body. It looked like a stretched out naked lank of a man. The monstrosity loped towards him through the fog.

"Enough!" Archer let his Beretta bark.

The boom echoed throughout the forest, and the creature stumbled with the impact but did not fall. No blood or bone showed itself in the fresh opening. Cold air wheezed through the wound like an open airlock. After a pause, the beast moved towards the gunman once again.

Archer finally freed himself of his nerves. He turned and dashed down the pavement. Whether that thing followed or not was impossible to see through the fog. Nonetheless, he ran on forever until he saw the *NO ENTRY* sign on the side path he was hoping for. It was a dirt road the led up a hill and deeper into the forest. But it was the only marker of civilization he could find.

Leaves tangled in a heavy wind swirled across the road as he ran for the dirt path. His heart leaped against his ribcage with every bound he made forward. Branches creaked and bent in the night. A harsh voice whispered behind him. Growing gooseflesh got the better of his breathing. Archer tripped over holes in the ground probably left by gophers or rabbits. His arms wheeled with stumbling steps and nearly brought him down. There was no way to tell if he was going the right way since everything looked exactly the same. All he could do was follow the trail.

"*I see you.*"

Archer sidestepped outstretched trees and bushes. The hills rolled suddenly and took him down and up at steep angles. Leaves rustled all around him like a wall of rattlesnakes. The path opened up ahead into another dirt road. This thin trail led over a low hill and toward a large fenced-in steel gate. The barred wall of metal had to have been twenty feet tall. Another large line of trees blocked any view of the opposite side.

He jumped for the bars of the gate and scampered up the metal. Hot breeze blew against his ear lobes and sweat thickened on his spine. A presence moved right behind him. He couldn't see it, but he felt it growing closer: close enough to blow breath on his neck. Harsh whispers tickled his eardrum.

Adrenaline fired Archer upward and he scraped against the point of the fence, slicing open his cheek. Hot pain overtook his fear for a millisecond before he threw himself forward. Archer slipped and tumbled the twenty feet back down. Hot air pushed against him before the dirt met his face head on. His left knee throbbed with the force. Before he could worry about any wounds, he turned around to face the gate.

A white, milky hand reached between the bars. Archer

jumped and yelled, rolling backwards in his askew balance. He banged his head against the grass. However, the appendage didn't come closer. Instead, it crumbled into the crimson mist not unlike dust.

He let out a hard breath, and felt his lungs pumping again. His knee still hurt, but his nerves settled. The monster was gone.

"Hey, boys," someone said. "It looks like our guest has finally arrived."

The trees rustled behind Archer. Several cones of flashlights beamed across his narrowed eyes.

Six men dressed in dark suits and black ties pointed barely visible handguns and automatics towards Archer. Their lights all shone over him, bringing his heart to his throat. These men were no good. He detected the whiff of dried blood on them.

"Well, well, well," the same person said. This crooked man carried an unlit cigarette in his mouth, and his unkempt blond hair and wide green eyes unsettled Archer. "It's not every day you get an intruder that's also a guest. Seems like it is the end of the world, after all. You're late, Mr. Archer."

The lights shone brighter as the sextet converged on the sprawled out Archer. He raised his hands in surrender.

"Late?" Archer said. "I'm early, if anything. I was supposed to be here tomorrow morning."

All six men looked to each other before the crazy one spoke again. "Get up. We're seeing the big man."

They seized Archer's arms and forced him to his feet. One man with a vertical gash across his lips and piercing ice blue eyes went for the intruder's coat and removed the Beretta from his holster. It took a moment before Archer recognized this thug. This was the big man from the odd dream he had earlier.

"I've seen you before," Archer said.

The large man sneered at him and pushed him forward. However, he never said a word. The two beside Archer wore their black trilby hats pressed low but made no reaction as they dragged him onward. The blue-eyed man receded to the back of the group as they marched through the trees.

First, Archer had become trapped in some disease-ridden fog, then he was chased by some strange monster, and then somehow ended up captured by a man he saw in his dream. This night was not going well.

One thing did keep him going, and that was the fact that this man was with Ariane in that dream. If he was alive, then she had to be, too. Archer didn't come to this meeting for nothing. His fiancé was waiting for him.

A spark of hope lit in Christopher Archer for the first time in months. Now all he had to do was get out of here alive.

CHAPTER II
Meet Your Maker

Archer's knee felt like oblong shards of glass had been rammed through it, and yet there were no markings or visible scratches on his flesh. Not even his pant legs were torn or scuffed. Then, just as soon as it arrived, the pain vanished like a bad nightmare. The men on either side of Archer pushed him forward regardless, but he couldn't help but think it bizarre.

Compared to everything else he'd been through, however, his knee was the last thing on his mind.

The flat path led through a thick tree line, and despite the unrelenting rouge fog sticking to them like stink in a barn they pushed on with assured steps through the nearly invisible trail. These guards had clearly passed through here many times before.

"How did you get in?" the one on Archer's right asked. "Where is the way out?"

"I woke up in the woods, and my car wouldn't start. What are you talking about? Way out of what?"

The crazy one growled. "Shut up, both of you. Franco, he doesn't need to know about anything. He's just Mr. McKinney's guest, not a park ranger. Archer, don't speak unless you are spoken to."

"Don't mind Doyle," the man beside Archer said. Franco's starched black hair shook awkwardly with his strained chuckle. "He just wants a smoke. It's been a dog's age. We could all use a day off. Overtime isn't worth this."

Each of the six men was troubled in some way. Archer could sense it through the way their twitching eyes darted across the sea of trees, and their breaths that jerked awkwardly. Their fingers fidgeted at random intervals. No one with sense would want to be trapped alone with them. McKinney had hired quite the crew.

On the other hand, the man with the scar over his lip, who someone called Charlie, had the least visible ticks. Aside from glancing at Archer from the corner of his eye he never said a word or made an odd movement. For a giant who lurched at his monstrous height, he moved as calmly as the eye of a storm. Of course, this man also had Archer's gun—his trump card of escape. Why would he be nervous? But then there was that vision. Archer would have to ask this thug about Ariane somehow. Hopefully, he could do so when he got away from these hooligans.

While Charlie unnerved him, and Franco made his eyes roll, Doyle made Archer's skin crawl. Of the six, he acted with just enough levity in his mania to disturb the disquieting atmosphere of the forest. At the same time he told the others to be quiet, he whispered jokes and spat when no one answered with a punchline. Any idiot who showed their back to this man was liable to get a bullet in it. Archer made a mental note to stay away from him.

The mansion stood out even more in the misty night air. A three-story monstrosity of old red brick and matching wood paneling awaited them. It housed thin purple and green vines like veins gripping the relatively recent rain gutters and large sliding windows with dark shutters lining each floor. The faint hint of mold and blood tickled Archer's nostrils again, and yet he saw nothing that would indicate the presence of either. So this was the place Ariane refused to talk about—*the* mansion.

They marched past a giant pit that had been dug in the front. He couldn't guess the size of the yard due to the mist, but it had to have been at least fifty yards wide. From the masked hole, the sounds of muttering and low talking could be heard. Archer was pushed past it through the wide archway of the mansion's front door. That was fine: he really didn't want to know what was down in that pit.

The stink of blood choked the entranceway, but again there was nothing to indicate any violence had taken place in this desolate house. In fact, the only oddness was the lack of any electricity. Two sets of pillars, set in rows of three, braced the giant thirty foot foyer. Old vaulted dusty hallways covered in old paintings and delicate vases forked off to the east and west with red candles, perched on tables and shelves, lighting the way. The group stopped in the middle of the cavernous lobby where the twin carved, gold-colored staircases swept up to the next floor, each set on either side of the group. This entire mansion was far too oversized for its own good, but at least Archer didn't have to be outside in the fog anymore.

Instead, the oppressive weight of a tradition, traveling back in time to when simple farmers in the fields worked for the lord in the forest mansion, stained the air of this place. Those farmers changed and bent with the times, moving to cities and towns and building their own farms far away from the hustle and bustle of urbanite hell. Archer had known such things before in his wilder years. This mansion remained untouched in the fog as if abandoned by the passage of time and societal progress. It was like walking into a forgotten past.

"Upstairs," Doyle said. "Franco. Williams. You come

with me. You rest of you return to your posts. You never know when *they'll* get in here."

The large Charlie looked back on Archer with a curled lip of disgust, before he disappeared into the red tint of the second floor with the other men. Archer was grateful to at least be rid of that monster, though he still had questions for the behemoth. Doyle made some sort of hand gesture to Charlie as they walked away, and the big man reciprocated.

Archer didn't want to know what these lowlifes were up to. He tried to keep his expression flat and pretended he saw nothing. "Expecting other guests?"

"We would be so lucky."

"Excuse me?"

"Never you mind. You're wanted upstairs, Archer. Follow me."

Whichever door wasn't shut revealed clean white sheets overlapping the drapes to the outside windows. Red splotches of candlelight shone out of a few of the rooms along the second floor. Dust mites and particles tickled his nostrils and the taste of ash swam across his tongue. This mansion hadn't been cleaned in a very long time, and yet it didn't look very dirty otherwise.

The group winded up the staircase ahead to the third floor to yet another wide barren set of halls. Archer was beginning to think this journey would never end when he was brought to a room on the far right end of the center hallway. The large wooden doors creaked open and the odor of burning flesh struck him. The polished shelves and vacuumed carpet betrayed the sight he saw next.

Tall arching windows, the only ones Archer had seen without curtains, cast dark crimson light across the desk at the edge of the room. The lone occupant sat beside his lurching shelves of dust-covered books and didn't react as his visitors reported in. Two sets of old Middle-Age armor sat propped on either side of his desk. Archer had seen this geezer before—he was the old man in that earlier dream. The deep pools in his eyes reminded the visitor of Ariane.

This old man sat in front of a burning candle with his hand perched on top of it. The skin smoked and sizzled as the geezer waited for the group to pile into his office. When they closed the door, he finally perked up.

Joseph McKinney's suit was as crumpled and stained as the rest of the men's clothes were. The geezer wore no smile on his thin and wrinkled face, not even the faintest indication of politeness and poise one of his stature usually exuded. He did not spare Archer even one sideways glance, instead focusing on his own sizzling skin.

Doyle stepped to his boss's side. "We found this one jumping the fence, sir."

"Judging from his clothes and the imbecilic look on his face, I'm assuming this is Christopher Archer. It took you quite the time to get here, didn't it, young man?"

"I'm early," Archer said. "Despite being in a car wreck, I'm here hours before our scheduled time. You have a signal out here, right? My phone is dead."

McKinney threw his own phone out on the desk. "Give mine all you've got, Archer. It's dead. They're all dead."

Archer took him up on his offer but found McKinney was telling the truth. More dead ends. He slammed the phone back down. Everything was going wrong.

"Great," he said. "Now I've got to hoof it to the nearest town in this fog."

"Are you this dense, young man?" McKinney rotated his hand over in the candlelight. His expression remained stone-faced as his skin smoked. "That's no normal fog out there. Surely, you must have seen something else in your journeying. You did hop my fence, after all."

Archer remembered the doppelganger, the voice, and the purple thing in the mist, but decided not to bring them up. The last thing he needed was to get involved in McKinney's games. These types were always up to no good, just as Ariane always said. He needed to keep his eyes on the prize and get to the point.

"Where is Ariane?" Archer asked. "I'm not here to play with you. Tell me where my fiancé is."

"Don't speak to me as if I owe you anything, Christopher Archer. I brought you here out of nothing but goodwill, and the hope you will make up for what you did. She would have wanted it."

"So you did bring her here! What a bastard you are. Do you think you can just kidnap someone, fake their death, and get away with it? Hand her over. I'm taking her out of this hole."

"You can't go, imbecile. You're trapped here now. We all are. I brought you here to make a deal, not for you to push a helpless old man around."

Archer pinched the bridge of his nose. "Enough of this. Tell me what you want, McKinney."

"I want to get out of this fugue state of misery, Archer. This prison is endless torture with no way out. I want to be able to escape, and I need you for that. Ariane always trusted you, which means I can trust you. At least, for this task. There is a *being* out in that forest we mistakenly unleashed. You might have met it. We need to destroy it so we can escape. For that, we need your help."

"You have guns. Just shoot it. Your men had no problem almost shooting me." He decided not to tell them his own results in trying to shoot the creature. They didn't need to know anything.

"It's impervious to typical weaponry. I'm sure you know this. Ariane trusted you with something, didn't she? Do you have it on your person?"

The back of Archer's neck broke out in gooseflesh as he thought back. He did not actually remember much before waking up in that car, aside from Ariane, though the memories slowly returned. His parents, his old jobs, his wanderings, none of it was very special or out of the ordinary. Nothing, that is, until her. All he could focus on was her face. That would never fade. The rest of it didn't matter as much as she did.

But he couldn't let Joseph McKinney know any of that—not the man who kidnapped Archer's fiancé.

Archer's hand slid into his coat pocket and found the small vial brushing against his right hand. A possibility existed that this was what McKinney wanted, but it was just a charm she left her fiancé. No chance would Archer ever part with it. This was the last thing she left him. For now it was safer to play dumb.

"I don't remember much. I think the car accident rattled me a bit."

McKinney blandly nodded, still refusing to look at him. "Take your time, young man. It isn't as if you're going anywhere. Doyle, take him to his new room."

He snapped his fingers, and the two thugs grabbed Archer and pushed him towards the door. But they were stopped when Ariane's father suddenly interrupted their exit.

"Did she tell you anything about her family before you last saw her?"

"The only thing she ever told me about you was that she hated her family, especially her father. I can see why."

"You do not know me," McKinney said with a huff. "There are few things I detest more than white wine, dry weather, and spiders. Disrespect is one of them. Show your elders the courtesy they deserve."

"You're Joseph McKinney." Fragments supplied by memories of Ariane floated through the void inside Archer's head. She never said a whole lot about her father, but it was enough. These memories weren't much, but they might be useful. "A man with connections who prefers to keep himself away from the limelight. I recognize you. Your daughter changed her name to get away from you, and judging from what I've seen, I can't blame her."

"Guilty as charged, rodent. But you can call me Mr. McKinney. My first name is for my friends, and those I respect, of which you are most definitely not either. However, that is a curious moniker you've got there, Mr. Christopher Archer. I feel as if I have heard it before."

Now he was playing with his guest. Archer was no one, and the old man knew it. "It's a common name. You must be confusing me with someone else."

"Possibly, you are nothing, after all. Nonetheless, perhaps I can interest you in a job? How are you with a shovel?"

"Ridiculous," the man beside Archer said. "We have more important things than playing with—"

McKinney simply raised his right hand and man fell silent. "*Don't interrupt.* Now please, *Christopher*, tell me why you bothered to come here. You seem to think my daughter is alive, even though I know you were told different."

He considered telling the geezer about the weird dream he had in the woods but decided against it. There was no sense in offering useless speculation to someone like McKinney. "I just want her back."

The old man pointed to the window behind him. "Do you see the blood red sky and forest? It looks like that all the time now. Every day and every hour."

"No, it's not." Archer rubbed his cheek, attempting to

18

remember what just happened mere hours ago. "The fog only rolled in over half an hour ago or so when I drove into these woods. Good weather for a drive. It was clear outside not that long ago."

"That was half an hour of your time, Archer." McKinney gestured to the men around the room. "We've been trapped at just after midnight of July 12th (I suppose it is the 13th now) for what might be years. The weather never changes, and the sun never rises. No one comes in, and no one leaves. We're sealed in this never-ending torture."

Archer sighed, scratching his cheek. "Enough of this nonsense. I didn't come here to be made fun of."

"You keep brushing at your cheek. Did you hit it on the way here?"

Archer had almost forgotten about striking his face on the fence earlier when escaping the monster. He ran his fingers across the wound and found . . . nothing. No pain remained, and no blood gathered at his fingertips.

"I thought I did," he said.

"That's because you're trapped in here with us. Wounds always heal. Always."

"Enough with your fairy tales, McKinney! Where is Ariane?!"

"Think about it, rodent. Why would I fabricate all of this? Did not the weather change all too suddenly when you woke up here? You saw that monster, I know you did! I assume it also tried to take your form. Hours before you were scheduled to arrive, a meteorite, red as raw meat, broke through the clouds and hit the forest. That is when this place fell to madness."

"And it just happened to land as I was on my way here."

"You passed through the barrier, I suppose." McKinney looked him over as if he expected Archer to give him something. When Archer said nothing, the geezer continued. "No one else comes up the mountain road except to visit this mansion. We won't get any other visitors here, because no one can get through the barrier. Not until we break it. Do you understand yet? You cannot leave. None of us can."

The insanity of this old man could not be explained with rationality. Whatever McKinney did in these woods had brought a dark beast out of hiding, terrorizing anyone unlucky enough to come through. Regardless of whether he was telling the truth or not, it remained clear that there was a presence in this place. Monsters shouldn't exist, and yet Archer knew they did.

"A temporal anomaly," Archer said. "That's what you mean? That meteorite took you out of time and space. You probably think the monster must have come from that so-called space rock, too. We're locked in here with that freak until it dies. Is that it?"

McKinney laughed. "You appear to believe this all too readily. Why is that?"

"I'm not fully convinced." Archer couldn't even convince himself that this was real, but he believed it. What choice did he have? None of this made any sense. "You say you've been here for a long time. If that's the case, then why haven't you starved to death?"

A sudden weariness overtook McKinney like a man up for days who longed for rest. He fell back into his chair. The geezer then closed his eyes as if nostalgically remembering days of sunshine and tranquility from his misspent youth. "We can't eat. We can't sleep. We can't tire. Everything is stuck as it was the moment that meteorite hit. Nothing ever changes. It is quite an exhausting predicament . . . in a different sort of way."

"Then you brought me here to die with you."

"Quite the opposite! You are the first living being to breach my property in . . . however long it's been. Not even animals live in these woods. That monster devoured them all. It had more than enough time to. You won't see so much as a rabbit, or a spider." He sighed as if a weight had lifted from him. "It is just us remaining. I don't tolerate trespassers normally; but these are extenuating circumstances, and who knows how long it will take before it gets strong enough to breach my property. It is nothing short of a miracle that this being has not gained enough power to manifest itself inside here yet. That is our ace in the hole! We need all the help you can give us to slay the monster and escape."

"If you think I can lead you through that red forest and by that *thing*, then you are grossly overestimating how much I value my life and yours. How in the world do you figure to get out of here, McKinney? Don't think for a second that I buy that convenient meteor nonsense. You aren't telling me everything."

McKinney laughed again, but once more without any mirth or malice in an empty joviality. There was no meaning behind the cackle, and Archer was beginning to believe there was no meaning behind the man. This demented old codger simply got in over his head with . . . *something*, and now he wanted someone else to clean up his mess.

"Archer, you really have no idea what you are in for. I would question if you are playing a part, but this would be an absurd character to keep up. When you hear voices at all hours, when the smells of rotting flesh fills your nostrils for no discernable reason, and when you taste blood when nothing is in your mouth, what do you call it? What do you call it when you are assaulted by nothing?"

"I would say it's insanity." Archer gazed to the crimson darkness outside the window. "As long as you promise to hand over Ariane, I'll do whatever you want."

"I don't think you quite know what you're asking," McKinney said. "If you get involved, you will be brought into the fold. Permanently."

"Whatever you're hiding better have been worth all of this. I'll only do it for Ariane."

"Stop saying her name!"

The hairs on Archer's neck trembled as if he were being watched. He turned from McKinney toward the door where he saw a thin face peeking through the small opening. It was a young woman with golden-red hair, beautiful lips, and the deepest blue eyes he had ever seen. Except that he had seen them before. It was her—Ariane!

Archer rushed toward the door, but she disappeared as quickly as she arrived. The men pulled him back, but he forced his way through their hold. He finally leaned out into the hall, but no trace of the young woman remained. Only the dead air of the mansion stared back at him. All that kept him company was the candlelight shining in the musty halls.

McKinney was laughing behind him again. "Is there a problem, Archer?"

"No," he said under his breath. There was no sense pushing it with Ariane so close. "Nothing at all."

"Good."

Doyle and his men once more seized Archer. He was their prisoner now, but he hardly cared. With Ariane nearby, nothing else mattered anymore. She was so close. But why did she run from him? And what was she doing with that big oaf in his vision? He didn't have the complete picture yet.

McKinney said only one more thing before turning away to the window, but it would stick in Archer's head, just as that vision of Ariane would. It was a cryptic phrase that made no real sense, and yet suited this depraved old man perfectly well.

"Once we bring it to life, we can do anything. We can even slay Satan himself and storm heaven in his place."

CHAPTER III
Blood Mansion

Harsh breeze blew against the mansion wall, disturbing Archer's concentration. No leaves rustled outside the second floor window, and there was no sign of life in the woods beyond the barely visible guard fence. The wind wasn't coming from anywhere at all. It was as if it were pouring out of, and returning to, the void.

That didn't bother Archer so much. He had worse things to worry about.

Archer had been left in a cavernous dust shaft of a room like every other one in this blasted mansion, but at least it allowed a moment to think. He needed it after all the madness that had just occurred.

That girl in the hallway looked almost exactly like Ariane, but it couldn't have been her. She was dead. But a speck of hope remained in him like a lone candle burning in a blackout. He never got to see the body, and McKinney was a liar. She had gone to the hospital for a checkup, and never came back. It was an aneurysm they said, and only family could see the body. They wouldn't let Archer in, leaving him out in the cold just as he was when he first rolled into town. But now there was a possibility! Perhaps she wasn't dead, after all.

But he couldn't quite hold onto that hope.

This was a trap designed by Joseph McKinney. Several guards even waited outside Archer's room to prevent his escape. Why would they need to do that if they were truly stuck in this forest like he said? That geezer wasn't telling the entire truth.

This invitation to come here, the meteorite, the red fog, and that monster, were all too expertly timed. McKinney was a schemer from all the rumors Archer had heard. Ariane always told him her family was a den of weasels. This felt exactly like what she warned him of. He just needed a clue to go on. What was really going on in this mansion?

However, he knew none of McKinney's mongoloids would tell him anything. There was also no way of getting answers from that monster, so only one path remained open to Archer. The meteorite, if that's what it was. Archer paced the small room and let the dry air choke a cough out of him. How could a mere meteorite cause this to happen? What exactly was it really?

On his earlier trip through the hall he took notice of an ajar door and the edge of a bookshelf inside the attached room. It was the only other chamber aside from McKinney's office that had more than one candle lit inside. There had to be a reason for that.

Archer tried the door to his makeshift cell and learned what he'd already figured: locked. With the guards outside his room wouldn't even be worth trying to make a break for it. He quickly moved to the window and gently pried it open with a tiny creak. It slid open and allowed a punch of humidity to smack his cheeks. The red fog waited for him outside. Before he knew it, Archer was out on the window ledge, heavy air weighing against his dry skin.

The third floor's height normally would have made it

hard to see the ground at night, but there was another factor preventing visibility; that blasted fog clung to not only the horizon but to the base of the mansion like a humid swamp. It didn't help being so late either. The ledge was nowhere near as frightening for him as the image of whatever would come out of the dark mist to pick at his corpse should he fall down there. Sweat dripped down his growing goosebumps. Had the fog grown thicker? He hoped it was only his imagination.

Archer sidled to his left along the thin ledge. Despite being barely a foot wide, he tried to avoid looking at his shoes to see how steady his steps were. Anything to dodge looking at the drop. Warm wind kissed at the gooseflesh on his neck with every move he made. It took a good minute before Archer reached the target window sill two rooms over.

He tugged at the stuck window. The stiff frame refused to budge. He groaned as he pushed and shoved at it, careful to avoid making noise. The wind whispered in his ear as he fought with the window. It was starting to form words. The presence wanted him to look down into the fog, to whatever waited to swallow him whole. He wouldn't give that voice what it wanted. Instead, he yanked at the window harder.

With a violent pull, it cracked and swung open, almost taking him backwards into the void below. The voice cheered, begging him to join it down on the ground. His arms spun like a windmill before he caught the inside of the sill. He braced himself before pulling his unsteady form inside. The bear rug rushed to meet his face. Thankfully, it muffled his weight enough that there was no reaction from the outside hall. The wind suddenly ceased blowing the moment he touched down.

Archer sat up and rubbed his sore jaw. Low voices whispered out in the hall. It sounded like McKinney chewing out one of his men. Archer carefully approached the door to the hallway and slid it shut. Finally, he was alone again.

Dust and cobwebs caked the corners of this study. The rank stench of mold did not help. This room had not been used in a dog's age, probably not since long before they became stuck here—if they really were trapped. This made the still-burning candles on the large carved desk twice as strange. A wall of books awaited ahead on the other side of the room. Two sets of armor sat on either side of the door out to the hall. Only the oversized bear rug and non-functioning lampstands decorated this study otherwise.

He combed through the book shelf, removing the tomes and scanning the pages. Minutes ticked by in his tired brain as he ruffled through the volumes. Nothing prevented one of those guards from finding him in there, but he needed at least one hint before he escaped. He couldn't leave empty-handed, not when Ariane could be in trouble.

Finally, he found a large hardcover slab clocking in at over eight hundred pages. This book on Celtic legends had some pages torn free. Archer had never been one for myths, but it had to be important if it was so manhandled compared to the rest of the tomes on the creaky shelf. He jiggled it free.

The table of contents and glossary allowed him to check what pages were missing. There was one on a spear used by a man named Lugh and a few others about witches and fairies. He didn't find anything inside about meteorites at all. But, *a spear*? What would a man need a spear for in a world where guns exist?

Archer blandly glanced around the room. He pinched the bridge of his nose in thought. There was no theory he could nail down here. This entire situation just looked like a glorious mess; the ravings of a loon.

Yawns fought their way out of him. Archer needed rest. But he couldn't sleep until he got something out of his trip to this dead-end.

He tried to bury himself in more of the books but found nothing he could use. Whatever McKinney was up to, it wasn't here.

Archer thumbed through a work on Welsh legends when a strange sensation fell over him. His urge to yawn faded. He wasn't the least bit tired anymore. Now he was filled with a vague sprightful energy . . . and a subtle hunger. The appetite of a wolf had taken control of his gut instead of the exhaustion that had been tugging at him seconds earlier.

Come to think of it, the cheek he thought injured was now perfectly fine. Had his fatigue departed for the same reason? Had he been healed of his tiredness? Could McKinney's crazy story have validity to it? He had been right about the smell of blood and the monster.

Archer ignored the thought and continued digging. This insanity wasn't worth contemplating now. He soon found a tattered journal amongst the books. Inside was nothing about McKinney's daily life, but plenty of random accounts of strange and paranormal events in this mansion over the generations since his family had built it in these woods. Voices heard on the wind, faces seen in the reflections of the windows, and strange rank smells wafting down the halls when nothing was around. These accounts went back to the 1800s.

Archer's stomach growled again. The last time he ate had been at a diner just off the highway. When was that? About three hours ago. But had it really been three hours? He shook his head. McKinney's madness was getting to him. A sudden craving for a well-done steak attacked Archer. The succulent sirloin perched in his thoughts like a hungry vulture, begging him to swoop in to eat it. Saliva dripped down his chin. He frantically rubbed it off. Why was he thinking of this now?

The doorknob to the hall turned, and Archer quickly

slammed the book back into the bookcase. Too long—he'd been dawdling too long. He crouched down behind the lone desk. Silently, he waited for the door to open.

The shuffling of shoes across carpet followed by a light click of wood kept him alert. Only two sets of steps had entered the room.

"What's taking that damn Eye so long?" McKinney asked. "The basement affair was ages ago now. I figured it would have made some move by now."

Doyle grunted. "No idea. You have the pages, sir. You'd know."

"Shut up, Doyle." McKinney moved towards the bookcase and struck something Archer couldn't see. "I'm dealing with enough problems. The men are right on the precipice of madness. It's a miracle they have held on this long. Hopefully, Archer's arrival will satiate them a bit longer."

"They eat, sir. You just don't want to know what they eat. As for me, I've been holding out hope for one meal in particular. Any problem can be conquered with the promise of a full stomach. But I'm getting off track. What is it that Archer has that let him in here? All I found was that bottle in his pocket that had pieces of metal in it."

"Those are the shards we've been waiting for. You didn't take it off his person, did you?"

"No, you told me to remove nothing but his weapons."

"Good. Then it's all ready to begin. Once we get Maurice out of the hole, we'll start. He keeps trying to take a piece out of Reynolds, and it's far past the point of being acceptable."

McKinney appeared to swipe something from the shelf, and the two of them moved towards the exit. The man behind McKinney paused for a few seconds. He mentioned smelling something, and Archer froze. The old man fell quiet in response, but it felt like ages before they finally moved again. The door shut behind the pair, and Archer let out a hard breath.

Their heavy steps thumped down the hall. Finally, the quiet of the night returned.

Archer slid out from behind the desk and stretched. He moved to the shelf, scanning it for whatever McKinney had taken. As he ran his finger along the spines, Archer muttered the names of the books in an attempt to remember what he had just looked through moments earlier.

Suddenly, light burst through cracks in the bookcase. A panel slid out from one of the volumes. He shielded his eyes. Before he could decide to hide, a woman told him not to move. There he focused on the book-spine-sized opening in the wall, and the familiar face that stared him down.

Her curled fire-red locks and bright blue eyes were like looking at a living photograph. Her perfumed scent drifted through the opening, momentarily choking the hunger out of him. From what he could see, she wore a simple green dress with a matching short-sleeve top. The red hue of the midnight mist made her white skin look almost see-through. It was Ariane! She really was alive.

"Ariane!" he nearly exclaimed. "You're really alive! Why did you run from me?"

"You're Christopher Archer," she said. He winced at her voice—he hadn't heard her in so long. But . . . it sounded slightly off. What was different, he couldn't make out. "You're her fiancé. I am Matilda McKinney, Ariane's sister."

Ice entered his veins. That was a blatant lie. "She never mentioned any sister."

"She wouldn't," the liar said. Her voice hitched with an odd strain. "We haven't spoken since she left home three years ago. How long were you engaged?"

"We were together two years." He tried to stop staring at her, but it was difficult. It had been far too long. She was the spitting image of Ariane. She had to be her, but why would she hide it? Did McKinney do something to her? Maybe this was a test. He decided to play along, for now. Whatever got her out of here was good enough for him. "She went for a checkup at the hospital three months ago. I was told she died suddenly, an aneurysm. But no one would give me any information, saying her family had already claimed the body. They blocked me at every turn, and then the geezer calls me for a meeting here out of the blue. What did the old man do all this for?"

She swallowed the words on the tip of her tongue before starting again. "My father had been watching her for some time. When he learned about her appointment, he made his move, greasing the right palms and donating the right amount to the right people. His men grabbed her and shipped her back home."

"Oh? Is that why the hospital gave me the run around? Is that why everything related to her disappeared from her apartment overnight? Is that why I had to hire a PI just to find out the name of the punk that was following me for two weeks after she vanished? Is that why lawyers have been threatening me for months? You tell me. Where is she, *Matilda?*"

"It's complicated."

He stared down at her through the cracks in the shelf. For a moment, his hunger subsided. It took everything for him to stop himself from pushing his way through and embracing her in his arms again. "Tell me where she is, then."

"You're going to want to go to the basement for that."

"This isn't the first time I've heard about this basement. I want an explanation. At least, you can give me something, *Matilda*. Your father is far too shifty to trust. Are you a liar like he is?"

She smiled sadly. "I'm sorry all this happened to you. It would have been better for the two of you to stay away from here and live your lives. But it's too late for that now."

"Okay," Archer said. He leaned back and waved towards the book case, avoiding her gaze. "What are these for? What is your father trying to do? Give me an answer."

Matilda sighed, before looking down at her feet. "I've been hiding in my room for so long now. Talking like this is too risky. Papa's men should be passing down the hall on patrol soon. They'll hear us. Go back to your room quick before they notice you are gone. I'll unlock it. Then you need to get to the basement. I'll tell you whatever you want when we get there."

"I already came this far." He didn't want to trust her, but his options were otherwise limited. She needed to tell him the truth. Why was she lying like this? It didn't square with what he knew about Ariane. She would only do this if what she was hiding could hurt him. But what could be worse than losing her? "You need to tell me everything then, okay?"

"I'll go ahead. Meet me on the bottom floor behind the kitchen. Follow the right hall beside the atrium. It's easier to sneak around alone here . . . even if it's riskier. You'll see what I mean."

"Ariane never mentioned you," he said. "But you look just like her. Why would she never talk about her family?"

"My father isn't . . . the warmest person. Seeing me reminded her of worse times. She blamed me for not steering Papa away from his . . . hobbies. It's too late to do anything about it now."

"It's too late for a lot of things, Ariane."

She paused, not looking at him in the eyes anymore. "Keep quiet in the halls. They travel in pairs. The next patrol should be around in the next five minutes. Hurry up. Once they pass, then you can go for it. Watch out for the big one named Charlie. He's vicious."

"He looks it." Archer sighed and rubbed the bridge of his nose. This was all starting to exhaust him, even if he seemingly couldn't get tired. "Listen, whoever you are, or whoever you think you are, I'll tell you this much. Ariane was grateful to be away from her family, but she was more grateful to be part of a community that appreciated her. Every day with her was an adventure, and whatever cynicism she might have had vanished by the time we decided to get married. She moved on beyond all of this. You should follow her example."

Her lip trembled for a split second before curling into a sad grin. "Thank you, Christopher."

The Ariane doppelganger closed the panel and left him alone in the study once more. Her scent vanished with her exit and so left the memories of his lost fiancé. Finally, he breathed easy. Women had rarely unsettled him as it was, but this one being so much like the woman he had lost managed to get under his skin. This one's scent was of one more of roses and less of the light French perfume his fiancé tended to always carry. Perhaps she wasn't Ariane after all?

No, that wasn't possible. She must have lost portions of her memory, just like he had. It was this phantom world that messed with everything. Soon enough she would recover what she lost, just like he had. This would all make sense when they got back home again.

Though he had been with Ariane so long, he realized he didn't know everything about her. What exactly were the secrets this family held that she wanted nothing to do with? She never told him anything. But now she was gone, and they took what remained of her. He didn't believe *Matilda* for a second when she said she was her sister. That didn't wash with everything else happening here. If her sister was here, then why was Ariane nowhere to be found?

Archer tried the door and found it locked. Just as expected. Instead, Archer moved back for the ledge.

He sidled over the abyss, careful not to look down. And yet, as he moved he could swear he heard a wet thump echoing somewhere in the night. Archer attempted to ignore it, but his brain kept trying to puzzle this madness out. It was rhythmic thrusting, like a knife coming down on a butcher's table. A low voice whined in the night. Sweat pooled on his brow. He just had to get back to the room. As the striking noise pitched louder and louder in his ear he could hear a whimpering voice gagging underneath the repetitive hits. It was a woman.

"I see you."

Archer threw himself back into his room and shut the window behind him. After catching his breath he stumbled to the door. Whatever that disturbing clatter was outside, it had to be another trick. That thing out in the mist was still trying to get to him. Archer tried the door and found it unlocked now, just as *Matilda* said it would be. He slid it open and peeked out into the hall.

He spied the red moonlight piercing the crimson fog to shine across the empty crimson carpets of the wooden floors. No one walked the halls. Where were the men Ariane mentioned? Was he outside that long that he missed them? Perhaps she lied. No matter how long he waited, their patrol never came by.

The ever-blowing breeze and voices in the night rattled against the mansion walls like the wailing cries of another world. He didn't want to know what it was—he just wanted his fiancé back. Quickly, Archer slipped through the doorframe and snaked through the hall. He kept down low, his

34

steps gliding along the nearly invisible floor.

The groaning mansion creaked under him. Its scent was of an open grave. He couldn't help but get the impression of a dirty past buried in so much dust and dirt that no shovel would ever uncover the remains. The weight of this place pushed down on him, just as it had on his memories. Whatever ghosts roamed this mansion from an abandoned past would hopefully never fall upon him like they did the rest. Archer had enough obstacles of his own to deal with.

Soon enough, he arrived at the open staircase highlighted by the stained moonlight. Distant creaking floorboards broke the silence as he stared down into the dark swirl. Eventually, they too faded.

In the cavernous foyer, he took in the sights again. Raised ceilings carried over dirty carpeting, paintings, and tables, where vases sat with immaculately placed red flowers inside. He sped past pillars scattered about the opening and toward the wide open hallway to his right. A large spacious archway waited ahead with a door flapping loose from its hinges. He had finally reached the kitchen.

Beyond the kitchen, he noticed a dead-bolted door at the end of the hall. It must have been the one that lead to the basement. A hard stench of rot punched his sinuses. Whatever was down there stunk worse than the blood and decay that lingered in the rest of this mansion. He needed something heavy to break that lock. Perhaps Ariane had the key.

A soft sound rustled behind him from the foyer, but it quickly died. Footsteps? He had almost forgotten about the sentries. Archer ducked into the kitchen before anyone became alerted to his presence.

He lightly pushed open the wobbly kitchen door and held back an impressed whistle. Pristine granite countertops, mahogany tables and chairs, and gorgeous matching cabinets pulled his eyes across the broad darkened space. The lack of electrical power and cleaning made it look as ancient as everything else he had seen in the mansion, only being lit by a lone candle perched on the counter. Still, a hunger clung to him. Perhaps he could finally get a bite.

The fridge had no power, of course, but he still looked inside regardless. His stomach sank back against his spine when he saw what was there: or rather, what wasn't. The food had been taken, as were the condiments, butter, and garnishments. They had emptied the fridge.

He swore and slunk into a kitchen chair. Why would anyone do that? The realization bit him like an ornery hornet. They wouldn't, unless they really were trapped here. The food had been eaten ages ago.

Archer needed his Beretta before he could proceed further. Being outgunned and unarmed meant being little more than becoming future fertilizer. Even if he made it into that basement they would surely not hesitate to end him when they caught up. Then again, they might not catch him. Once he had Ariane, they would sneak out of here, and he would leave them all in this mansion to rot. He just needed for her to finally get here . . .

Archer had no idea why he was brought to this place. McKinney was not looking to reminisce with someone who knew his daughter. That much was clear. This mist over the forest was dubious timing for such a meeting, on top of it. More and more it seemed that McKinney's ridiculous story might have validity to it.

Archer scratched his chin when his ears cocked at a sharp thumping outside in the hall. He spied a glance out the askew kitchen door. Boots creaked on the floorboards as a guard moved towards the kitchen.

"I could eat a bear raw," Doyle said.

Archer silently scanned the room. There was no other exit, nor any place to hide. The line of cabinets under the sink beside the dishwasher were all too small for him. Nonetheless, staying out in the open wasn't an option. He looked to the wall length cabinets to his left and glanced inside. This was more like it. The insides had also been cleared out like the fridge, leaving enough room to fit someone like him. Carefully, he climbed inside the cramped space and closed the cabinet.

His head narrowly missed slamming against the ceiling. This tiny space meant he would have to remain still. As he settled in, Archer peeked through the thin crack out into the kitchen.

There was a bang like heavy wood against the wall. The door was either thrown open, or kicked in. A low growl filled the kitchen.

"Damn," Doyle said. "Where's the food? Damn."

Hard stomps crashed across the tiles toward Archer. Doyle paused at the sink and turned towards the supply cabinets, muttering to himself. He marched in Archer's direction.

"No, wait," Doyle muttered. "Not that. *No, no, no.*"

Doyle turned around and threw open the fridge. The stooge paused, perfectly still for what felt like hours. He whined to himself, softly at first, until the low groans became shouts.

"Nothing, nothing, nothing! No! I need *something, something, something*. I should have eaten that bastard whole. Damn, boss stopping me. Damn. Why can't I just? Why can't I eat? Why did I take this job if I can't eat when I need to eat? Damn, damn, damn. Boss got us trapped in here with his stupid whore. I'd eat her. Yeah. Soft skin. Tender. Beats barking at the moon."

Then Doyle suddenly ceased speaking. He stepped over to the sink and leaned out towards the fogged window.

His breaths fell hard and steady like a wolf waiting for a meal, as he otherwise remained speechless. Sniffs sounded from his otherwise silent frame.

Archer waited, his legs numbing. The panting and raving had vanished, but Doyle's silence was worse. What was he doing? Archer's knee twitched, and he caught it just as it brushed the cabinet door. Spasms crawled up his leg, and he narrowly avoided hitting it against the wood. He couldn't wait forever.

"*Are you there?*" Doyle asked.

Archer froze. His breaths stopped with his racing thoughts. Silence hung in the air. Doyle had heard him. But, no, maybe he hadn't. Crazy loons always talked to themselves. Perhaps he hadn't noticed anything. All Archer could do was keep still as his muscles trembled.

"It isn't my imagination," Doyle said. "I know you can hear me. They can always hear me."

Pain shot through Archer's cramped knees. His escape options were narrowing by the second. He tightened his hold on his kneecap.

"I've been waiting for you. The Eye. It's close, so close. Can give *it* to me. My food. *Damn, damn, damn.* Stomach needs food. Boss needs to kill the whore. Should send the food to do it. No one will miss them. No one will see them. The Eye might. I hate the pain—it always makes me hungry."

The creep's heavy breathing returned. A low whine mixed with a growl from Doyle's gut was all that could be heard in the kitchen now.

"Outside, huh," he mumbled. "They're just outside. But you're inside. Right here. And you're mine." Doyle's hungry tone twisted into a mocking laugh. Scorn and bitterness seethed from his barking madness. "*I smell you.*"

Large fists slammed against the countertops. The lunatic kicked the cabinet beside the dishwasher. In one motion, Doyle ducked down and swung open the dented wood. He pulled out a thin arm attached to a woman. The woman Archer was waiting for struggled as Doyle forced her to her feet.

"Your scent is unmistakable, *Princess*," he said, with a sneer. "You think I could forget that, being here for as long as I have? Hiding in your castle tower away from the riff raff: you can't run from us forever."

The woman who called herself Matilda yelled toward her aggressor. "Let me go, Doyle! You have no right."

"I have every right, woman. It's *your* fault we're here. You owe me. A bite will do, then you can cry to Daddy for all I care. What's he going to do, kill me? Fat chance!"

Archer reached into the dark where a small pile of broken pots and pans remained beside him, and pulled out a steel slab. It would have to do. He slid free of the cabinet and stalked towards the large man that kept his back to him. The woman yelled at Doyle, not even seeing Archer's approach.

She whined. "I only wanted to remember the smell of food. I know it's not there, but I needed to believe it was for just a moment. It's been so long."

"You're crazy," Doyle said, "and I would know. You can't eat. I can't eat. We're never escaping this hell. But I can make you pay for Daddy's, and your man's, mistakes. I'll get some blood in me!"

Doyle tightened his hold on her slim fingers and brought them to his mouth. She began to cry out when he seized her throat with his free hand. She gagged, and he licked his lips.

"I was thinking about your fingers, but your ears will make a good starting place."

"*Stop!*"

"Don't worry, they'll grow back."

Archer brought the pan down on Doyle's skull. The resulting crang sang inside the kitchen, and Doyle reeled. He turned and Archer slammed the steel object against his nose. The psycho spun to the floor and landed like a heavy sack of stones. Doyle's crooked nose on his unmoving body was a tough sight to see. At the very least, there was no blood.

"You," the woman said. He looked into her diamond-hard eyes. "Thank you."

"What are you doing here?"

"There's no time, Christopher. You better get going before he wakes up."

"He's not getting up. Were you watching me? I thought you wanted to meet me here."

"It's complicated. Look!"

Doyle's nose popped and slid on his face like an inflating balloon. The bruise discoloration faded away, and his skin regained its dirty color again. Even the spittle on his nose receded back into his tongue as if the air frightened it. Doyle blinked awake and slowly stood back up.

"Who hit me?"

Before anything else could happen, Archer rushed him. He seized the goon and tackled him to the ground on his stomach. A handgun flew loose from Doyle's coat, and Archer's gripped loosened on the pan. Doyle thrashed about, asking his perpetrator's name.

Archer grasped his dropped pan. He brought it down on Doyle's skull over and over. The crunching gave way to a series of soft squishes. Eventually, the body stopped twitching. However, there was still no blood.

"Run, Christopher!" the woman said.

"Why? Is he going to do reform again?"

As if she willed it with her words, the wounds on Doyle's skull began to disappear just as they did moments before. His skull solidified and the skin reattached itself. Was he immortal?

"Run before he finds out it was you," the woman said. "Don't worry, I can handle him."

She stood over the twitching body and picked something up from beside it. Archer didn't notice what it was as he was too busy moving towards the exit. There was a bang from the gun in her hand which caused Doyle's corpse to jerk.

"That should take him a bit longer to fix. Hurry back upstairs, Christopher."

"I'm not going to leave you here, Ariane."

Heavy creaking erupted throughout the mansion. Men shouted from floors above.

"Yes, you are," she said. "If they catch you down here they're going to do worse to you than what you did to him. They won't hurt me—I'm Papa's daughter. We'll figure out another way into the basement later. Get out!"

The bullet wound on Doyle's back was already beginning to heal. Archer didn't have a choice but to trust her now. After all, she had been here much longer than he had. The last thing he needed was to be caught here and like this. Archer still had questions but now wasn't the time to ask them.

"It's a promise," he said.

Archer hurried out into the hall and rushed back towards the atrium. A cavalcade of steps thundered down the large staircase at the end of the foyer. He could barely make anyone out as the figures descended through the hazy night. The guards rushed towards his direction. Archer ducked behind one of the large pillars and waited. A group of two tore down the hallway behind him. Four more men poured down from the winding stairs at the end of the room and also dashed by his hiding place.

Running guards burst into the kitchen and yelling

soon followed. Several of the sentries shouted out Doyle's name. Archer used the distraction to head up the stairs towards his cell of a room. The stench of blood filled his thoughts and his headache pounded with his shoes against the carpeted floor. He threw open the door to his room and clicked it shut behind him.

That was when it hit him like a wrecking ball against a crumbling building. Doyle wasn't dead. McKinney wasn't lying. They had really been trapped in a world of undeath. They had eaten all that food ages ago, and now they had nothing to eat. At least, *not proper food*. As he thought about the possibilities, his heart skipped a beat.

This *couldn't* happen—but what if it *did?*

Those horrendous and impossible thoughts filled his head again as he sat on the creaking bed. He parsed them out as he let his nerves settle.

Why was McKinney's group stranded in this mansion to begin with, and what was that thing out in the woods? A familiar icy chill ran through his veins when he thought about it. He knew that monster, though he could not understand how.

Voices slowly approached from down the hall. He sat up. They were coming for him.

Archer clutched the small bottle in his pocket. Those tiny metal shards were inside. Why did McKinney want these? He couldn't possibly guess the reason. Ariane left these to Archer. No matter what happened, he would never give them up.

Archer wiped the sweat from his brow. The doorknob rattled.

McKinney, with three men, entered the room. Screams bellowed from somewhere inside the mansion behind them, but none of the men flinched. Two of the lackeys rounded on

Archer and held his arms, forcing him still. They forced him closer to McKinney.

"I could have sworn the door was locked," McKinney said. He smiled. "Maybe my memory is playing tricks on me. It's difficult to hold your mind together when a constant weight is forcing it to bend. We're all going a little crazy. You'll understand, soon enough."

"What is that noise?" Archer asked. "What are you doing out there?"

"Change of plans, young man," McKinney replied, ignoring him. "We have to move the schedule up. The men won't last much longer like this, and we can't afford to play nice with a rodent like you. You and Ariane are about to have a reunion! Why do you look so distressed? I thought you wanted to see her again?"

"Somebody out there is screaming."

"Don't mind Doyle; he's simply broken the most important rule. My men are at their limits, you see. Only so much punishment can keep them in line if they have no hope remaining. But now there is hope! You gave it to them. Unfortunately, I can't afford to be polite any longer with you, rodent. There are more important things to worry about than your petty concerns with my daughter."

"She's my fiancé, and I'm taking her back. We have nothing to do with any of this."

McKinney lifted a handgun and forced it in Archer's mouth. "You'll see."

The weapon fired, and the fiery pain inside Christopher Archer's skull gave way to darkness.

CHAPTER IV
Spear in the Dark

The low lights of the library burned into the young man's temples. His headache flared as if a constant pressure had beaten itself into his brain. It had been a long week, and Christopher Archer just wanted some rest. Nonetheless, it was his day off, and he would get to read his book. He had earned it! He was so engrossed in his own problems that he hardly noticed when the woman approached him.

"Are you okay?" she asked. "You look like you've fallen off a truck."

He rubbed his eyes. "I've been there before."

"Sorry?"

"Nothing, never mind." He looked up from his book and saw the young woman glancing down at him. Her fire-red hair was tied in a ponytail behind her. She was slim with enough hip to turn heads. She couldn't have been older than her early twenties, same as him. Her sundress shimmered even under the artificial lights of this tiny small town library. It took everything he had to not stare too long. "I've seen you around town."

"You're new around here, aren't you? Mrs. Davis, my neighbor, says that you're a hard worker. You show up for the job, do everything you're asked, never complain, and quietly go back home. Christopher Archer, right?" She sat down beside him. "I'm Ariane Jones. Welcome to our tiny town."

He shook her hand. It was soft and small, but the warmth caused his heart to jump. He masked it with a laugh. "I already have a reputation, do I? It's nothing personal. I lost my family a long time ago. Being alone is something I'm used to."

"What are you reading, if you don't mind me asking?"

"John Carter. It's a series about a man who travels to Mars and marries a princess. And that's only the first book. A lot of people would just read it digitally these days, but I prefer holding things in my hands. Judging by the fact I'm here alone a lot, I guess no one else thinks that way. Do you read, Ms. Jones?"

She winced, but hid it quite quick. "Please, call me Ariane. And no, I've never really had much in the way of hobbies. Your book does sound very romantic."

He didn't want to say it, but even if there were rumors being spread about him, there were also rumors being spread about her. Jones wasn't her last name; she came here to escape from shady characters, and she kept to herself because she didn't want to talk about her past. Yet here she was sitting beside him. He didn't want to believe she was using him for some scheme, but he had no reason to ditch the girl. Besides, it was nice to have someone to talk to sometimes.

"How about you take home the first book, read it, then we'll talk about it next week? Sound good to you?"

It was a very long moment before she responded, as if she were reconsidering something. "I'd be delighted. What is the first entry called?"

"*A Princess of Mars* by Edgar Rice Burroughs. Ray Bradbury once said he inspired more boys than anyone else to become engineers and astronauts. I can see that. There's something magical about wondering just what is out there beyond what we can see."

"Who is this Ray Bradbury? Is he also an author?"

He laughed, despite himself. Once he started, he couldn't stop. It was as if a weight had lifted from him, and he just couldn't imagine feeling so light and giddy. She didn't look at him like she was offended, but more confused. He couldn't blame her when he didn't know why he found such a simple thing so funny. It looked as if she was well acquainted with patience. When he finally calmed down, he apologized to her.

"We've got a lot to talk about," he said.

His skull flared, and he screamed. Christopher Archer fell over, but he didn't hit the floor. Instead he landed in dirt. The buzzing sliced through his cogent thoughts and left him in agony. His eyes blurred, and the light from the library vanished with the memory.

The clink of a small object against cement woke Archer from his haze. The first thing he saw at his side was a spent bullet casing rolling across the dirty grey ground. His skull ablaze, he sat up, and the crushing pressure slowly left his head.

Faded light shined from over his shoulder. He could only make out the cold stone of the walls and the dug up concrete floor underneath him. Burning beams broke the quiet atmosphere, casting dancing shadows on the basement wall.

Now he remembered: he was in that mansion. They had taken him downstairs. The library was a dream, a distant memory. All of his fuzzed memories had returned, and now he recalled *her*. Archer would have rather that he continued to forget it. Thinking of her only hurt.

"There he is," someone said. "Now we can get on with this."

Three men in suits mulled by a set of large concrete stairs behind Archer. The steps climbed up to the familiar wooden basement door at the top. They brought him down here of their own accord? Archer climbed up on shaking legs.

"Hey," the man at the front said. This fellow was average height and build with bushy blonde hair and a matching mustache. "You must be Archer. I'm Miles. You've met these two?"

The second man was taller than Miles, built far too big. He might be mistaken for a marble statue if not for his pinkish square face that looked like it was carved out of a block of misshapen wood. His nearly shaven rust-colored hair was covered in a pork pie hat.

"Charlie," Archer said to the giant. "We've met."

The other man behind Charlie grunted. "I'm Len. Don't expect anything from big Charlie here. He's just here to keep you in line. We're going to be doing all the talking."

Len was slightly taller than Miles but in a dumpy way. His bulbous gut and balding hair almost made him comical. Archer recognized him as one of the men who found him outside in the woods. Through the dark, a glint appeared in his eyes when he smiled. Warnings signalled in the back of Archer's brain: Len was not to be trusted. The other two were comparatively harder to read—especially the one who never spoke—but this man wore his malice on his sleeve.

"Come on, pardner," Miles said. "You're coming with us. You want answers, you gotta get going. It's not that far, trust me."

At the edge of the basement, a tunnel had been carved into the wall leading down through a wide, chiseled corridor. Fluttering orange light flickered out of Len's torch to guide their way. The three men led Archer down the sharp angles of stone. He couldn't even begin to guess what they were doing down here.

Charlie took point while his allies walked beside Archer. The tall man carried a flashlight of his own and did not bother to slow his pace. Archer wanted to ask him about that vision he had back in the woods, but there was no telling if it meant anything, and the last thing he wanted was to help these suits. But why was Ariane with him in the dream? Archer bit his tongue. It would have to wait.

The faint scent of burnt wood assaulted him, followed by the stench of flesh. It lingered, even with no other living being in sight. Perhaps they had led him into an underground tomb of some sort. Perhaps they were preparing to bury him alive.

Archer checked his pockets for the vial. It had been taken. His breath jerked. He kept his poker face as they pushed him onward. He needed to get some info before they made their move. "How long have you been with McKinney?"

"I told you that we're going to be the ones doing the talking," Len said.

Miles laughed. "Ease up on the guy. He still doesn't know why he's here. That has to be annoying."

"Are you going to tell me?" Archer asked.

"Len won't, but I might."

"What about the big man?"

"Charlie doesn't talk to anyone. Can't. You see his lip? He had a bad time before we ended up in here. Shame it didn't happen to Len instead." Miles ignored Len's grumble, and continued. "Mr. McKinney has been planning this recovery mission for a while, but there was no guarantee it would work without the right person. He locked the basement and forbade us from coming down here ever since that meteor passed by. Who knows what we'll find in this hole?"

"You're not giving me anything, Miles. Does it have anything to do with Ariane?"

"There's nothing I can say. Of the three of us, only Len

was down here with Mr. McKinney before the door was locked. Don't know what happened since I was patrolling outside with Charlie. You'd have to ask ol' Len what happened."

Len said nothing. He marched onward as if he heard didn't hear anything.

"Anyway, I haven't seen her since we came here. Maybe she's hiding. I wouldn't blame the poor thing. I think the boss man and Len here are hiding something themselves, Christopher. I'm going to start using your first name, alright? Anyway, after they went down here, the sky outside went dark, and this strange meteor passed overhead. Then the mist came, and we've been stuck here ever since. Seems weird that Mr. McKinney would send you down here without coming himself. Whaddaya say, Len?"

Again, Len remained silent. If it wasn't for the thin beads of sweat forming on his thick forehead, Archer would have thought he wasn't listening.

Miles continued. "To be honest, Christopher, whatever gets us out of this hell is good enough for me. I'm starving here. You understand. Those of us who got to eat the food have it much worse, though, but it's still annoying. I'm seeing walking turkeys everywhere I look. Guess that's not so far from the truth, considering my company."

"Shut up!" Len shouted. He turned on the group. "None of you idiots understands what we're dealing with in this underground deathtrap. I'm here to guide you in and out and to prevent anything worse from happening. Keep quiet and move."

Archer's lip curled in confusion. "Worse happenings? Aren't you shooting your own men upstairs? I'm pretty sure I heard someone in the pit outside, too. I'd say we're well past the point of disaster. If I find out you did something to Ariane down here I'm going to kill you myself."

Len's hand went to his coat and then flipped it open. He drew his gun and fired it into Archer's head. Red crackles of agony blew Archer away. The sound made both Charlie and Miles jump.

Archer slammed against the side of the tunnel, splitting pain pulsating in his brain as a patchwork of black void and red mist spiderwebbed his vision. He slid to the floor and lost sight of the world.

Instead of death, a crashing impact rocking against his chest. Archer blinked awake at the new pain of being kicked in the ribs. He coughed and wheezed. The source of the kicks swore down at him as he attacked.

"*You don't get it! You don't get it! You don't get it!*" Len madly repeated, saliva sputtering down his lips. His stare could cut steel. "You have *no* idea!"

The large Charlie put his hands on Len's shoulders and dragged him off of Archer. That didn't stop the madman from screaming and thrashing in his hold.

"Ease up, Len," Miles said. "You did steal the poor guy's girl."

"I didn't steal anything! She was Mr. McKinney's daughter. He's the only one who really loved her, if you believe in such trite trash. You want to see the results of so-called true love? You're about to. It's just ahead. You'll see, you stupid, arrogant bastard."

Miles helped Archer back up to his feet, and the group trudged onward for only a little longer. Len kept quieter than Charlie the rest of the way. Only the flashlight and their footsteps kept them company. They soon reached their destination. Len was right—they did see.

A large grey altar awaited them in the center of a spacious cave clearing. The ceiling climbed up into an infinite darkness. Torches on either side of the altar burned forever just as everything else in this hell-world did. In the middle of the stone slab, a giant shaft stuck up into the air with the bottom a metal blade sunken into the altar surface.

That lodged object looked like a spear. It had been left here unattended. Len gestured for them to go towards it.

Archer slipped and slid down the groove in the dug-up floor before regaining his footing. Charlie motioned towards the dark ground underneath them. The two sentries both used their flashlights to check. A charred black crater with water-stained stones littered the indentation around the hundred foot opening. In the middle of these chaotic remains of crushed stone, he found piles of ash. Archer stepped over the mess and moved through the giant ditch.

The scent of blood strangled his throat from the inside. Suddenly, Archer thought of that horrific dark creature in the woods around the mansion. But he didn't need to be reminded of that beast. He needed answers.

The group met at the altar, and Charlie removed the vial from his coat pocket. Neither Len nor Miles said anything when he gave it back to Archer. Len gestured to the weapon embedded in the altar. Up close, Archer could see it clearly. It was a spear with a pointed blade that looked perfectly pristine aside from a handful of chipped metal pieces in the center. Those indentations perfectly matched the shape of the pieces in the vial.

Len sighed. "You know how you managed to get into this unending limbo we're in? It was with those pieces. They can pierce anything. Mr. McKinney knew you would get in through the barrier with those. I'm not sure why he was so certain you would bring them here with you. Where did you get them from, Archer?"

"Not that it matters now, but Ariane gave them to me." She had wanted him to always keep them on his person.

But she never told him why. They were important and should never be left out of his sight. After she disappeared, he never once let them out of his sight. "She never told me these were pieces of a spear."

"That's not a normal spear, Archer." Len ran his fingers along the spear shaft and flinched. "It's one from legend—the weapon that slayed Balor and extinguished the evil of the Demon's Eye. We've tried to chip pieces over the years to study it, but it can't be done. This weapon is fortified by an intangible force. It's indestructible, and the blade leaves no bloodstains behind."

"Then Ariane shouldn't have had these shards to begin with."

"The only known fragments were passed down through Mr. McKinney's family. Rumor is they were broken off in the battle the legendary hero had with Balor. They still have magical properties, but we could never fit them back in. Only the wielder can do that, apparently."

"Magical properties?" Miles interrupted. He looked to Charlie who just shrugged back at him. "I suppose breaking into this empty limbo proves there's something to that. But it doesn't explain why *we* ended up in here, does it, Len?"

"Shut up, Miles. What matters is that the only one who can put the shards back can wield the spear's true potential. Mr. McKinney thinks that's you, Archer." Len tugged against the shaft, but the weapon remained lodged in the stone slab. "Now, you try."

"Try what?" Archer asked. "Are you insane?"

Len spat on the ground and folded his arms. Charlie eyeballed his cohort. Neither made a move from their stationary spots beside the altar.

"Forget him," Miles said. "That spear is a valuable treasure to the family, but it's never been used before. I didn't even know it was brought down here. Whether Len is on the ball or not hardly matters, but you might as well give it a go anyway."

"And I'm not going to be told what these shards are supposed to do," Archer said.

"Will it hurt you to try?" Miles shrugged. "If not, then enjoy more of what you got upstairs. That is, if that thing in the mist doesn't find its way in. I see it move along the fence perimeter every now and then. Only a matter of time before it gets in. Just put the pieces in the spear. We've got nothing to lose."

Miles wasn't wrong; Archer had nothing else to go on. Was this spear fashioned from the legend, or was that legend true in some capacity? All myths had one foot in truth, but after this mess he landed in, it looked as if they were closer to being waist deep. The spear awoke a longing in him, as if he knew it from somewhere.

A strange tingling sensation ran through Archer, and odd thoughts popped in his head. This spear was a part of him. He *knew* it. Christopher Archer was allowed to be alive for this moment. It was ridiculous, but he believed it. That missing part of him could finally be filled.

Archer ran a hand along the gold rivets and sharp edge of the spear point. Its dark bronze head and haft of rowan told him it was a weapon of some weight, but that was easy enough to fake. People like McKinney dealt in forgeries all the time. What made Archer believe it was more than a mere weapon of war was the heat warming the shaft. His fingers were drawn to it like the right polarity on a magnet.

Thanks to the books upstairs, Archer knew a little about the story. Lugh was known for slaying the god with the Poison Eye: Balor. The spear contained great power, known for being able to burn anything to cinders when held by great warriors. A lot of questions popped up as he thought about this weapon. Balor was slain, but what happened to Lugh? What was this spear created for? What was it made to do?

Most of all: what force powered this weapon? McKinney wanted it, after all. And what did Ariane have to do with a spear? None of this added up right.

"*Christopher*," it called in the back of his mind. His name echoed repeatedly. "*I see you.*"

Charlie rotated his hand at Archer in a hurrying gesture. It was time to get on with it. Archer agreed with them. He had been waiting his whole life, after all. Wait, that wasn't true. Was it?

Archer carefully removed the three shards from the vial and placed them in the grooves of the metal spear. They sunk right in like puzzle pieces, and a flash of red glare emitted from the blade. He blinked through the sudden blindness. The spear had changed! He checked, and the cracks had vanished, filling in the formerly empty spaces. He couldn't tell where he had just put the pieces in.

Heat grew in his chest. They were meant to be together. "*I see you.*"

Archer lunged forward and clasped the weapon. Stone groaned and crunched as he drew it back with his full strength. Muscles strained, but he refused to let go. After a few seconds, the spear gave and split the rock of the altar as he freed it. He lifted it high in triumph.

Flaring bolts of pain shot through Archer's hands and inside his nerves to his eyes and brain. He dropped to his knees, and his mouth gaped. It *hurt*. The world was lit ablaze like fire and frozen like ice with both sensations burning simultaneously through his body. Words attempted to form on his tongue, but nothing came out. His bones and very being buckled as if dragged through a black hole before being crushed into nothing.

Archer thought he heard someone yelling in his ear, but he wasn't sure it wasn't his own screams echoing off the stone walls of the cavern.

The world around him warped and twisted, and Archer fell through the ground like it suddenly vanished. He plummeted into a darkness of eternal night with stars watching over him. Numbness and fear washed across his nerves. Death licked at the back of Archer's neck and chills hugged at his spine. He was left with a single thought.

Had the spear betrayed him?

Christopher Archer sunk deeper into the darkness. He could only think that he was forgetting something—someone. Perhaps the spear wasn't the only traitor here. Why did he even come to this place?

"*Wake up, Christopher,*" it had said.

When he finally opened his eyes he realized he was no longer in the cavern.

He was no longer even on planet Earth.

CHAPTER V
Alien Mausoleum

If Christopher Archer was dead, he wasn't in any afterlife he had ever heard of before. Cold steel sent frost under his sweat-soaked back and through his shirt and coat. Chill slipped through his bones and woke him up. He looked out and found the underground cave had vanished.

A blanket of stars overhead presented him an ending view of outer space. Rain poured from the empty sky where no clouds existed and soaked him to the bone through his coat. This wasn't Earth—it didn't even look like a planet. The air he breathed was the only thing that gave him grounding to believe he wasn't actually drifting in space.

While the entirety of his body ached as if it were a punching bag that went too many rounds, it was his right hand clasping to that spear that burned the worst. His palm sizzled and throbbed so badly he was convinced it had been severed even while looking at it. But he couldn't let go of the weapon. His fingers held to it tight despite his protestations.

A shot of dread caused him to panic. He pried at his right hand, but it was no use. He choked off a curse when a whisper called out to him.

Tall blockages wrapped around his position not unlike

a hedge maze, darting off in random directions and prevented him from seeing any clear path forward. Instead of branches and leaves, they were merely hunks of black metal that towered at over twelve feet tall. Thankfully they at least shielded him from most of the cold breeze slipping through this labyrinth, but it still stopped him from knowing just what was waiting out there.

Black rainwater enveloped the dark onyx-colored metal of his surroundings. The only reason he could even see all this was the lone light illuminating from the steel tiles underneath his drenched boots. Beams of brightness shone up from below as if someone had installed motion-sensor lights in the complete opposite place they should be. Nonetheless, they beamed through the hard ground and lit up wherever his feet stepped.

Finally, he gathered the courage to look closer at his right hand. It looked as bad as it hurt. Black burn marks tattooed his tightened fingers and blackened nails. Steam seeped up from his stiffened hand. Burning heat cooked his palms, along his arm, and up through his shoulder.

Archer still wanted to let the spear go, but every part of him refused to listen to those pleas. This weapon was a part of him now. He needed it, and no one would ever take it from him, especially not McKinney or his cronies.

A raspy whisper slithered into his ear through the rain. It beckoned him to come forward. Archer slipped into the cold downpour and held his spear close. This voice was someone new.

He crossed through several paths until he reached an opening in the unkempt metal maze. No other sign of life stirred through the soft storm. The rain stopped falling as soon as he left the labyrinth behind.

The courtyard before him held a sextet of stone statue gargoyle creatures that towered up to thirty feet tall. They were placed on either side of the narrow path before him. At the end of the road, an impossibly tall mausoleum with a forty foot metal grating at its opening stared down at him. The gate swung open at his approach despite no one present to move it.

The mausoleum towered at over two hundred feet tall and contained sculptural relief he couldn't make out due to the monstrosity being as black as the sky itself. How did he not see this structure from back in the maze? All he could make out was a faint outline of dark stone and metal clashing against the downpour.

A ripple in the onyx wall to his right allowed a man to step through. At least, it looked something like a man. The near seven foot figure wore a grey robe with an oversized hood over its head that rolled over its limbs. The being kept itself at a safe distance from Archer.

"*Welcome, wielder,*" the robed creature said. It didn't sound like it spoke those words, but thought them into Archer's head. "*It has been eons since we last met one of your kind.*"

Archer winced at the shot of pain flowing through his right hand. "You brought me here."

"*Few are willing to spill what blood is required in order to wield that weapon. You are holding it, which means you were called to obey its wish. That is, if you desire its power.*"

"A sacrifice? Don't lie to me. There was no corpse where this spear was found. No blood, either."

"*It does not merely murder. It consumes. That was the true purpose behind its design. Only beasts of war could create such a thing, though it is far beyond your race of men.*"

The realization hit Archer, and his lip trembled. The inevitability his mind had fought to accept was now crushing in on him. That woman in the mansion was who she said she was—she wasn't Ariane. The longer he held the spear the more he knew that woman wasn't her . . . because she was in the spear. Archer felt her there, whispering in his ear. She was dead.

Archer's legs gave out, and he fell to all fours in the rain. Dizziness and fatigue consumed him whole. Sweat dripped down his neck as his muscles trembled. She was dead. She was really dead.

He threw up. His arms trembled and water fought its way through his tear ducts. The smeared world made it difficult to concentrate on anything but the reality blooming before him in the storm. Eventually, he found his voice again.

"McKinney used this thing on Ariane. He murdered her."

"*And yet you wield it instead of him? Curious. The spear does not recognize his right to the sacrifice. It is a folly on his part. Few men seek the spear's power without throwing themselves and their kin away.*"

"He used it on his own daughter." Archer was hardly listening to this alien any longer. None of this mattered. Ariane really was dead and gone. The ache tightened in his chest and made him wince in growing anger. He wiped his smeared vision clean. "That son of a bitch."

Boiling rage built inside Archer. Just when he thought he might see her again—just when he thought she might not be gone forever—McKinney took her away from him yet again. And now she would never return. All for what? A mere legend. He wouldn't even be able to give her a proper burial or see her body. Archer bit his lip so hard he hardly noticed the blood leaking down his chin. The fire in his hand felt like little more than a dull warmth now. It was nothing compared to his billowing fury.

"I don't want this spear," he said, his voice hoarse with anger. "Take it away."

"*It cannot be done. You have fulfilled the requirements, and now you must use it. It will not allow you to walk away,*" *and no other can use it. Not until you perish from its flames."*

The last thing he wanted to think of was this blasted spear. McKinney had used it to sacrifice his own daughter and, because it didn't allow him the power he wanted, decided to use Archer as a guinea pig instead. How many lives would he throw away to get this damned weapon? Archer considered running it through his own body. What did he need this thing for, anyway?

But still that constant reminder pricked at his nerves. He would never get her back.

However, he *could* get McKinney back. A mad joy leaped into his heart and caused him to grin in a way that would sicken the sane. If that old geezer wanted him to have the spear then Archer would show him the spear. It would look perfect rammed into McKinney's heart. The burning in his right hand subsided as he thought of the ways to butcher that murderer.

"I can use this spear for anything?" he asked.

"The weapon was fashioned by those who wished to make a sacrifice for ultimate power. A berserker's dream. Whatever you use it for is your choice—it only desires blood for fuel. You can even choose to walk away if you do not wish to return to your world."

"So we aren't on Earth."

"Very far away, in fact. I am not speaking your tongue. You would not understand my language without telepathy. I am here to instruct the wielder on what power lies in his fingertips. It is a true honor. Should you wish to leave your home, I can guide you to a world where you can rule as a god."

That thought sounded very enticing, Archer couldn't deny. Doyle, Len, McKinney, and the rest of those monsters deserved death. Whatever that red mist gathering around the forest was could eat them alive for all he cared. They were nothing to him, or anyone. Criminal scum deserve death. They summoned that hell so they can choke on it.

But he also thought of Matilda, Ariane's sister. How much of this did she know about? She did help him back in the mansion, after all, despite not needing to. That couldn't have been a ruse. Could it? Yet still she was trapped in limbo with flesh-eaters and a monster closing in on her. She didn't deserve that fate.

As easy as it would be to just abandon her with the rest of them, he couldn't do that. She was still Ariane's sister. She wasn't one of *them*. For all he knew, McKinney could use her in the next experiment and cause this to happen again. Archer wouldn't allow that to happen.

"Where did the red mist come from?" Archer asked. He forced himself to stand again. "Tell me."

"*The darkness you've seen is the lingering remains of the one sacrificed, her sorrow and rage has become one with the fabric of the hidden space. If it is not stopped it will consume everything into it, even the wielder of the spear. That is, unless the Eye devours them first.*"

"The Eye?"

"*It was summoned, was it not? The one who is responsible for your presence here is certainly a greed-filled fool. He believes he can wield both the spear and the Eye? That will not end well for him, or your world.*"

"Who cares about that geezer? You said Ariane is still out there. That's enough for me to go back."

Ariane wasn't really dead, after all. His smile spread so wide he thought his mouth would crack. Of course, it all made sense! She hadn't been entirely taken by this spear. She was still out there in those woods. He could return to her! A twisted joy glowed inside his heart. Untold happiness returned to his beaten and bruised heart.

"*You've made your choice,*" the robed thing said. "*Go to the mausoleum and destroy the capstone. It will unleash the hidden power . . . but beware.*"

"Beware?"

"*Once the seal is broken, the Eye will hasten its approach. It will react using the greatest fears of those who unleashed it. This is the warning before it strikes. The Eye will never stop until the wielder is exterminated.*"

"I'm already dead without her. Show me where I need to go."

"*Very well. Enter inside and run the spear through the statue on the second level. Once you pierce its heart, the sealed power will rush out, and then your true trial will begin. You will know the capstone when you come across it.*"

With the instructions finished, the robed alien stepped backwards into the black space and out of existence again. Archer was left alone in the abyss with his smoldering spear. But the weapon no longer bothered him.

Ariane was still beside Archer in the spear and back in that limbo, at the same time. As confusing as that was to understand, it hardly mattered. She was still with him. Archer had a chance no one else would ever get, and he would use the chance to make them all pay. She would understand.

Inside the damp mausoleum, he felt eyes on him from every angle. The cold black stone from the shadows betrayed a structure that had been built long ago. The creatures carved in the walls and on the statues looked like those he had seen in old bestiary books back in school. They had awkwardly-shaped long limbs, talons curved at wrong angles, thin faces like lizards, and eyes as wide as owls. Their marble-like eyes pierced passersby as if they were prey. Archer quickly stepped past them.

Somewhere in the dark, he heard a vague wind, whispering voices from far away. Their cries kept his nerves on edge.

Archer traversed grey stone stairs into a large open room which had a forty foot statue on a platform in the center. An engraved hunk of stone below it spelled out a word in a language he could not decipher. A warm front blew inside his soul—this was the capstone. But what a capstone it was.

The shape of the statue reminded him of a hunched muscular man-shaped figure with goat legs and horns. It almost reminded Archer of a Minotaur except that its face was exactly that of a man's and no different from his. It might have been some sort of human in its life, but now it lay in this grave, forgotten and alone. However, it was missing a crucial feature. This monster had no eyes.

Then it hit him—this was Balor's grave. This was the very one from the legend he discovered back in the study. The spear wanted him to relive what Lugh felt when he used it so long ago. This was the blood it wanted so bad. The remnants of this monster would satiate that urge.

And Archer would oblige.

The spear heated up as he brought it back. The thought of slashed open flesh made his mouth water. He knew it was coming, and the spear wanted him to feel every inch of it. The pain in his arm was gone now, replaced with a gentle pinpricking of warmth. The numbness allowed him to move the weapon as if it were an extension of his body. He imagined it as a third arm, and he moved it just as easily.

Archer lunged forward with the spear. It stabbed into the statue, and stone split with the hit. The tip of his weapon glowed red as the rock structure crumbled around it. Cold air gushed out of the opening. Hard heat built in the pit of Archer's stomach as the realization set in on him—he was free! The spear sizzled as the last of the stone rubble fell to the ground, leaving little but smoking ruins. The chill dissipated.

For a second, he thought he saw a spark like electricity inside the statue, but it disappeared as quickly as the bloodlust in his bones did. The spear suddenly grew so hot he thought his hands would melt off.

Archer dropped to his knees as the heat overtook him. A bright white light lit up the corners of the black pit of the alien mausoleum before extinguishing as quickly as it arrived. He questioned if the spear might have even absorbed the brightness and the dark into itself.

Why not? It could do anything.

The world rippled and faded around him. Once more, he saw cave walls and the outline of three men standing by a broken stone altar. The flashing of the torches allowed him regain his bearings. Archer had been thrown back into the mansion.

Before he could feel any sort of relief or joy returning home, a wave of small ripples ran along the shadows around the circumference of the open cave. He thought he saw a tiny creature the size of a small dog squiggling out of the dark corner and tearing down into the forking tunnels. Its long, thin legs clicked against the rock walls.

Was that a spider?

CHAPTER VI
Limbo's End

Weak torchlight cast thin rays of brightness through the darkened cavern. For a moment, Archer had forgotten that mausoleum and what had happened there. The pieces snapped into place, and he suddenly remembered what he was tasked with. The air in the cavern vibrated differently, though he couldn't say why. Perhaps because he now knew what it was that he had to do.

"What are you jumping so suddenly for?" Miles asked. He straightened his lapels and brushed sweat from his forehead. "It's just a spear, right? You've never seen those before?"

Len scoffed. "I thought you didn't believe in that mumbo jumbo, Miles?"

"Never mind that. The man just suddenly jumps after grabbing a spear. Freaked me out. With all the other insanity going on around this place, I wouldn't have been surprised if he melted out of nowhere. We should get out of here. I'm getting a bad feeling."

"Wait," Archer said. "What are you talking about? I've been gone for a while now. I left here to some sort of alien world."

Miles looked to Len then back to Archer. "No, my

friend. You were here the whole time. You touched that thing and then not even a second later, you jumped back like you were being shot at. Aliens? Are you joking? I can't even tell anymore."

Miles and Len watched Archer as if he was just let out of a straitjacket, but Charlie kept the same hard stare as always. The silent behemoth sighed before checking the gun at his side. Whatever reason it was that Charlie hated Archer, it transcended the impossibility of the situation they were trapped in.

Despite knowing he had vanished from this place to that mausoleum, Archer still returned to this location exactly at the same moment he had left it. He hadn't been missing for even a moment. That place was certainly real, and so must have been that statue of a monster he destroyed. But that robed being said something else, right?

Yes. Breaking the capstone would unleash a monster. Was that a spider he had seen earlier? That thought caused his breathing to stiffen. The last thing he needed was more threats to deal with in this pit.

"Come with us, Archer," Len said. He drew his handgun on the spear-wielder. "Mr. McKinney's going to want to see this."

Archer tightened the grip on his weapon. Time to bluff and stall. He needed to see if that spider really was real. "You never showed me where Ariane is. Fulfil your end of the deal."

"*Our end*?" Len sneered. "There is no deal here, Archer. You were brought here because you were needed to play a part—we all were. Now to finish what you started."

"Easy!" Miles interjected. "We don't need to get nasty about this. That isn't gonna help anyone. We're *all* stuck here, right? Let's just keep calm."

The spear's heat shot into Archer's bones as if someone had turned a furnace up. His arms jerked in a spasm. "Give me one decent reason I shouldn't gore this trash right here."

"Gore me?" Len said, his weapon still aimed at Archer. "I'll shoot you down long before you reach me. You lead the way out, now."

Archer growled. "I'll send you *somewhere*, champ. Now, answer me. Which one of you was it?"

"I said to move!"

"Which one of you killed her with this spear?"

Both Miles and Charlie paused at his words, but Len didn't budge. Instead, he cocked his weapon. The former two goons glanced about in confusion amongst each other.

"Charlie," Miles said. "You didn't see a body when you were sneaking around down here, did you?"

Charlie shook his head. He ran his fingers along the surface of the battered altar. The tall figure sniffed the air and grimaced.

"*Sneaking around*," Len repeated. He leaned towards them. "You two have been busy."

"It's not like that, Len. We've been here so long that we just wanted to know what was going on. Charlie's been spending some time with Matilda, but she wouldn't say nothing. He comes sneaking around down here, and we learn there is no sign of her sister anywhere. Where did she go? No one dies in here, right? We couldn't understand it. Meanwhile, that blood fog outside is getting worse all the time. The voices are getting louder. You understand, Len. You have to want to get out as much as we do."

"I want names," Len said. "How many of you were in on it?"

"Enough!" Archer roared. "Who killed her with this spear? Was it you, hair-trigger?"

"You still don't understand, do you, Archer? The spear can only be awakened by one who sacrifices everything to it.

He had no choice. He's lost everything else. She was all he had left."

"So why didn't he draw it out himself? Why couldn't he?"

"The spear can take all the sacrifices you can give it, but its power could never be unleashed without the missing pieces you had. Ariane took those when she ran away. We ransacked her apartment and found nothing. We never would have found out where they went if that neighbor of yours didn't tell us. Then it was only a matter of getting you here."

"Bunch of bastards."

"You wouldn't have come willingly if we didn't promise you your woman in exchange for those shards. But that's not important. What is important is that if you want to escape this place, we need that weapon to stave off the Eye. It's getting closer all the time, and now that you have revived the spear, it will speed up its approach. Put aside your emotions and do the right thing, Archer."

They used Ariane as nothing more than a tool. She was a sacrifice, and he was a guinea pig meant to take her place. McKinney found a way to get the spear without having to harm even a fingernail of his decrepit body. Once more the heat built in Archer's brain. The smell of burnt skin filled his nostrils.

Scratching stone echoed in the cavern. Those whispers from the dark returned to the back of his brain.

"Kill him! Run him through the heart!"

Miles grimaced. "Put down your spear, Christopher. We'll just handle this rationally. Let's go back up and chat with Mr. McKinney, then we can all get out of this nightmare in one piece. Isn't that enough?"

"I'm," Archer said, choking on the rage in his throat. Tears formed in his eyes despite how he usually fought them off so easily. They burned away before dripping loose. His whole body shook with a boiling fury who could no longer contain. "I'm going to kill everyone who took her from me. He threw her away for nothing. For a damn antique."

"You idiot!" Len yelled. "That's the spear talking. Don't let it control you!"

A small symphony of clicks clacked out in the cavern shadows. Both Len and Archer couldn't help turning towards it. Archer had forgotten about the spider! Small fuzzed-over bodies the size of footballs darted out of the dark ceiling above them and down the walls. Tiny hisses ejected from their mouths as they scampered towards the group.

Miles gaped. "Are those spiders?"

The fat arachnids trickled out from the black space of the ceiling, the infinite void above where nothing could be seen. Dozens, and then hundreds, of the little beasts, rushed down the wall towards the lone quartet of humans.

Len spun on his heel and fired at the eight-legged beasts. Bullets pierced flesh sending out gobs of neon green blood staining the jagged grey walls. Charlie and Miles soon joined him in shooting the monsters. Despite their bullets striking meat and the plentiful downed bodies, the tiny monsters did not stop advancing.

"Forget it!" Miles said. "We need to get out of here!"

Archer seized the flashlight from Charlie and tore backwards through the crater towards the opening they had originally entered from. The others' footsteps followed close behind him into the narrow tunnel, as did their many small enemies.

They flew down the path, shots firing behind them into the darkness they rapidly left behind. Hard breaths fell from Archer, and sweat streaked down his cheeks. That robed being wasn't lying after all. Were these the fears the spear unleashed?

But he wasn't afraid of spiders.

That was when it dawned on him. McKinney was the one who used the spear on his daughter. He was the one frightened of spiders. It wasn't any of these three goons—it was that geezer again.

"*Kill them. Piercing the heart is enough, Christopher. Kill them all.*"

Ariane's voice rang in his ears like church bells waking the damned in the underworld. His fingers involuntarily tighten on the spear. They would all burn.

Shouts from Miles broke his concentration. The man beside him screamed in his ear. "They're coming out of the ceiling!"

Archer checked his corners. Above, and to the right, and the left, sprinted spiders out of the shadows into the narrow tunnels. They leaked in like raindrops through a hole in the ceiling. Gunshots went off around him, sparking against the cave walls. The black tide of spiders fell upon the fleeing group regardless of their attacks.

His lungs stiffened, and fire erupted inside of his organs. The spider bites sent stabs of hot flames throughout his nervous system. The weight of the black arachnids pushed him to the ground in a heap. Inside his head, the voices screamed in tandem with the men behind him. This time, he really would die.

"*Kill them all!*"

Archer's fingers forcibly clasped on the spear, and he dropped Charlie's flashlight to the rock floor. With both hands, he swiped his weapon wildly, the rage pouring through him. Flames erupted from the spear, and the spiders before him squealed as they were incinerated in the attack. Archer twisted in a circle, gliding with the spear and slashing the air with tall orange flames that arched wide, scorching the side of the cavern. Blood boiled inside his skin as he attacked like a man possessed with rage and joy in tandem.

Despite his wild movements, the spiders continued to waterfall from the ceiling. No matter how many he murdered, they wouldn't stop dropping in.

The kindling heat rose with his temper. Archer jerked around to the tunnel behind him and jabbed into the blackness of spiders. A fissure of flames forced its way through the mass. Screams from the beasts followed. Streaks of fire burst along the pathway, catching the little bastards ablaze. The tiny dark beasties were instantly eradicated, and the tunnel filled with long strips of fire, staining the stone itself in an unending bonfire. A sudden ache flared across Archer's ribs, causing him to lose consciousness for a single second.

Len stood up straight, clutching his handgun and breathing hard. Despite his chubby frame covered in cuts and green blood dripping from the fresh openings, he looked much better than Archer felt. The goon grumbled to himself. "Where did those damn things come from?"

"They're here for me," Archer said. "They are part of the Eye, manifested to what the wielder is most scared of. Your boss's arachnophobia nearly got us killed."

"And how do you know that?" Len roared. He trembled from what could either be rage or fear. It was difficult to tell with Len. "How do we know you didn't cause that to happen?"

A large hand clasped Len's shoulder. Charlie breathed hard, and a gash oozed green liquid from above his eyebrow. The large man looked ready to collapse at any moment, but he still held his ally tight in his hold. He shook his head at Len.

"Get off me, Charlie! This bastard is the cause of all this."

A fire in Archer's throat caused him to gag and then

spit. Neon green liquid sprayed from his cough. His fingers felt under his shirt where his ribs flared. Black stains like charcoal painted his tips. Before he could worry about himself, he looked over his traveling companions.

"Where's Miles?" Archer asked.

Only scorched stone and a still-burning funnel of flames awaited the tunnel behind Charlie and Len. Torn pieces of a black suit and splotches of bright green liquid were all that remained on the floor. The spiders had somehow taken Miles.

"They got him," Len said.

Archer gazed into the black of the tunnel beyond the flames. Even if those things got Miles, they couldn't hurt him, right? No one here could die. That didn't explain the odd green blood dripping from his cuts or the blackened skin on his chest. Destroying the capstone must have done something to the limbo of this place when it allowed the Eye inside.

He checked his throbbing forehead where the spiders bit him and found more bright green blood trickling from the sores on his wounds. Bile rose in his throat. The bleeding wasn't stopping.

Loud squeals distracted Archer from his thoughts. The swarm of spiders had returned, edging along the fringes of the flames behind them. Both Charlie and Len backed away from the maddening group. Archer watched, allowing the realization to slowly hit him.

"They're scared of the fire," Archer said. "Better use this chance."

The group fled down the tunnel. They soon found themselves face to face with the exit. Archer shouldered the door open, and both Len and Charlie slipped past him and stumbled to the basement floor. More squeals chirped from the tunnel behind them.

With the heat in his fingertips, Archer struck the walls

beside the door with his spear. Fire scorched out of the cracks he created, swirling around the tunnel like an air funnel. The spider web of created flame climbed around the circumference and filled the pathway. Archer shut the door behind him. They wouldn't be getting through that.

The other two were already halfway up the basement stairs, and he chased after them. Archer huffed as the foreign blood continued to leak from his wounds. The skin around his fingertips was scorched black like his ribs. Did the spiders cause that, or did the spear? He would have time to deal with it when he got to safety.

At the top of the stairs, the group swung the heavy door shut behind them. Archer soon found himself surrounded by a dozen men with trained sidearms and automatics on him. Among their number, he noticed Doyle, several of the men he met by the gate, and McKinney. The only one missing was Matilda, and Miles, of course.

The old man looked the three of them up and down, his flat expression as empty as his the words he spoke. "You're alive."

"You sound almost disappointed," Archer said between breaths. His right arm trembled. Stabs of pain prickled through his radius and ulna bones. "What's with the welcoming committee?"

"Matilda is missing. According to those two idiots that were watching the door, she went down in the basement after you. Tell me where she is."

For the first time since Archer had arrived, McKinney showed an emotion that broke beyond the complete control of his burgeoning madness. The twitching of the old man's lips signified hate ready to explode like the fire in Archer's spear. McKinney called to the men behind him, and a chorus of clicks rang out from their firearms.

Both Len and Charlie watched their allies lining their shots at them. The chubby one with the big mouth gestured to the others with a wave of his hand. His shaking was quite noticeable.

"Look guys, I'm bleeding," Len said. His teeth chattered. "When this punk pulled the spear, it freed some kind of force. I felt it down there, and so did Miles before the spiders took him. Yes, giant spiders are down there. I don't know why, but—"

"Because your boss is scared of them," Archer said.

McKinney bit his lip. "Unleashing the true potential of the spear sends both hopes and fears out into the void when it consumes all else. The Eye certainly felt it. It will be on its way soon. We must be prepared."

"So you *are* the one who did it!" Archer felt that familiar hate boil inside again. "You sacrificed your own daughter to give the spear its power back. For what purpose? To break that capstone? What does it have to do with this *Eye* you keep mentioning?"

"She isn't dead, you cretin! She's there by your side, waiting for her father to join her in paradise. The only one who could unleash the spear was the one who sacrificed what was most important to them. I gave up my Ariane, and I still couldn't use its power—I couldn't even remove it from the altar. Before you arrived here, I thought that perhaps it wanted Matilda, too. Then I would have had to kill her, as well! Don't you understand my pain?"

"Fire isn't good enough for you, geezer."

"The Spear of Lugh and the Eye of Balor are natural enemies. The Eye was pierced by the spear and banished into the recesses of space, with most of its power sealed by said spear—that capstone you mentioned. At the same time, the spear was chipped and robbed of any use. Once one is awakened, so, too, will the other: opposing forces of destruction that no mortal man can stop. They had been lost for so long. Man can't stop them, no. But they can control them."

Archer's stomach flipped inside of him as he listened to this madman. "You're mental."

Charlie slowly turned only his neck towards McKinney, a wide-eyed expression dawning, most likely taking in this insanity for the first time. The other men even moved unsteadily, aside from the five closest to the old man, including Doyle and Len. There was a secret here that Archer, and many of the other goons, were not privy to.

McKinney babbled on. "Now that you've brought the spear back, we can face the Eye. Soon enough, it will be strong enough to enter into this mansion, aiming to consume those that summoned it to this world. Once it attacks, I will take control of both it and the spear. You've played your part as bait well, Archer. But you're in the way now. Hand over the spear."

Len chuckled. "I did what you said, sir. I brought him down there and got the spear. But what were those spiders? Part of the Eye? I can't stop bleeding. I thought we couldn't be injured."

"You won't stop bleeding," McKinney said. "Were you not paying attention to what I said? The Eye has broken the containment here. All bets are off. For a more important question: did not see Matilda in your travels?"

"There are some winding paths, sir." Len coughed more lime-colored blood. "You know that. Maybe she made a wrong turn chasing after us—if that's what she was doing. How should I know? You can't blame me for that."

"That is true, I can't. But I can give you a last chance. Take the spear from the rodent, and I won't put you in the hole again. We just took poor Doyle out not even hours after we took out others including Miles—pardon me, I forgot he wasn't here. Disciplining my men is hard, but it simply must be done. Do this right, and all is forgiven, Len. You know I keep my word."

"You—you do, sir." Len forced a trembling smile at his boss. Chuckles soon followed. "We'll be out of here soon."

"I never lie."

Len turned on Archer, his grin fading quickly to a sneer. His quaking right hand slid towards his inside pocket.

"Don't do it," Archer said. He showed his enemy the spear. "I will run you through."

"So what? You can't kill me."

Ariane's honeyed tones echoed in Archer's ears. "*The heart! Kill him. Kill him!*"

Archer winced at the voice. Why wouldn't it go away? "Back off, Len. I'll do it."

"Give it to me!" Len roared. The mad crinkle of his brow caused Archer to take a step back instinctively. Green liquid joined the spittle on Len's chin. "This is your fault!"

Len drew his handgun, and Archer rammed the spear forward with both hands. The tip split through the gangster's heart, piercing flesh and slamming him against the old wood on the wall. Len gagged, coughing neon green life force. A plume of orange flame erupted from the weapon and tore into the opening it had made. The fiery tsunami devoured the bastard's body. It soon consumed Len, cutting of his cries into the crackling flame.

The flame-engulfed corpse flopped to the carpet, still ablaze with his mouth emitting silent screams. The charred remains soon stopped moving and only the fire remained alive, greedily devouring flesh and bone. The smell of crisp flesh choked the air with the crackling pops of the pyre bringing the hallway to silence.

Within a couple of seconds of hitting the floor, the

flames suddenly extinguished, and all that remained of Len was a charcoal-black corpse without any defining features. Chatter filled the hall before the dead man crumbled to ash. Whatever remained of Len was fit for an urn.

"I killed him," Archer said, to no one in particular. A smile tried to force its way on his face, but he successfully fought it off. Ariane cheered in the back of his head. "He's dead."

Archer's hands crackled with shots of pain. A bolt of invisible electricity jolted his nerves. His heart jumped, and his blood froze. He just knew that more of his skin had been stained black, but he couldn't bear to look. Bile threatened to rise in his throat again. He closed his eyes to shake away the agony. Archer wasn't quite in control of his own body anymore.

In his mind, he watched a stranger from a first-person perspective. The host kicked a trash can over in an alley before closing in on a half beaten man in a suit shivering behind it. The bloodied and bruised victim begged and pleaded as the baseball bat struck the prey's teeth and crushed the cheek, spraying an arc of red spittle across the dirty alleyway. Archer, or the man he was inside of, swore at the victim for wasting his time and making him injure the loser. The boss was waiting for this attacker to return.

Then his host laughed, and Archer knew who he had become.

These were visions of Len. Snapshots entered his head like an old picture show as Archer struggled to free his thoughts from these invading emotions, too many different feelings and wicked ideas darted through him at once. Len had been eaten, body and soul.

But one thing was clear—the spear wanted more. That crazed hunger from before grew in his gut again, but it no longer desired something as mundane as steak or roast beef. Now it needed blood. *He* needed blood.

"*Kill him! Kill him!*" Ariane said.

McKinney shouted. "Shoot him!"

The men cocked their weapons and aimed Archer down. He moved to dodge, but it was too late. Their bullets tore into his flesh and bone, the raucous sound of gunfire breaking his dark thoughts and causing his entire body to dance against the stream of shots. His flesh parted, or at least, he felt it split, as stabs of agony rocketed through his circular system.

Laughter erupted far away from him. A deep guttural voice that sounded nothing like a human was filled with mad joy at the carnage. This was paradise.

Archer didn't even remember losing consciousness. Death wanted to claim him and, for a moment, he wanted it to take him. At the very least, it would free the tired avenger from this nightmare. Archer's cheek crashed against the charred carpet, the bright lime-colored blood still leaking from his old wounds. What would it take for him to die?

McKinney ordered his men to seize the spear-wielder. The abominable feeling in his chest took him into a deep sleep with words from Ariane he knew were meant for him this time.

"*Kill him! Kill him!*"

CHAPTER VII
Whispering Dead

Glass cracked, and someone swore. The sudden noise jolted Archer back to consciousness.

Sparks of agony sizzled in his brain. No matter how many times he tried to open his eyes, a new gunshot to the head dragged him to the brink again. Frustrated cries were cut off with his sudden death and revival, a cycle of needless carnage that kept him in a perpetual state of misery. Archer was far past exhausted with it all. It would have been better if he could just be allowed to finally die.

Memories of a man obsessed with perfection consumed Archer's fluctuating brain space. A quiet, calculating deviant named Len Daly stood behind his boss for over a decade, watching and waiting for his moment to get ahead. The betrayed and the dead lay in his wake, and more would fall on the road ahead. One day, this Daly character would be one to be feared.

However, that rat McKinney changed all the angles with the revelation of darker forces creating the rules of the game. Where the old man got his power, his iron fist control over the streets, and the odd aura around him, came from a place Len couldn't even imagine. But it was a power he would grab for himself. The first step towards this was to volunteer for everything asked of him, including sacrifices to higher beings.

Archer's mind crossed with the dying thoughts of Len, and he saw the future dead man seize Ariane and carry her down to her fate on that altar. He was there when the geezer murdered her.

For the first time in Archer's life, the thought of killing another human being made perfect sense, and the voice of Ariane playing in his mind agreed. She had the right to blood.

"Kill him! Kill him! I want his heart!"

Finally, Archer could open his eyes. He was leaning against one of the pillars in the foyer, surrounded by McKinney's men. His arms were locked behind his back, and his head sang like a wounded canary. He could only guess why they dragged him out here.

Several feet before him stood McKinney. In the decrepit murderer's hands, he held the spear and stroked the edge that had killed Len not too long ago. When he noticed Archer, he solemnly nodded at his prisoner.

"This is a good weapon, rodent. Even I couldn't imagine it was as powerful as that."

Archer's burning throat choked out a few words. "*Not yours.*"

"Considering this was made possible from my daughter's sacrifice, I'd say it is. You owe me, anyway. Both of the girls are gone because of you."

Archer coughed and spat to finally clear his throat. The sizzling pain punched at his mind. He grimaced. "You did all of this. If you cared about Matilda, you would go down there and find her right now."

"I will retrieve her soon enough. But as for you: you have worn out your usefulness. I hope everyone here takes in what is about to happen." He pointed the spear at Archer. "They are about to witness the Ascension."

Once more, glass cracked. Archer looked for the source and found it high above them in the foyer. The windows on the second floor balcony split and crunched. A wall of hard crimson rouge blacked out the view to the outside. If it wasn't for the men holding flashlights around the atrium, basic sight would be impossible.

"Do you even have a plan?" Archer yelled over the din. "The Eye is on its way in now that the spear is free. All these men, and you, are going to die."

The geezer shook his head. "Reality itself bends to the one with the strongest will. This weapon proves it just as history does. Even an amoeba like you was able to conquer this relic. Can you imagine what someone of my stature will accomplish?"

The waves of pain washed over Archer again. The lingering thirst for blood and gore left him dry. A sudden weakness caused light-headedness and a weightless sensation in his bones. Had the spear done this?

"You have no idea, McKinney. This was worth throwing away Ariane for?"

The old man's face crinkled in a hard rage of lines and sharp teeth. "Don't ever say her name!"

"She's dead because of you."

"She's with me now! All that awaits you is the burning depths, rodent."

McKinney jabbed the spear into Archer's heart. Piercing pain pumped through the injured man's softened body. He lit up in a bonfire just as Len did. Archer's agony was swallowed by the fire that soon consumed him whole. It was all over.

The flames cascaded over Christopher Archer, a blinding heat that pulverized flesh and bones. A wall of red rage and death was all he could see in the dancing fire. But despite the scorching pain he felt a renewed sense of strength inside. The building pressure released itself with a guttural roar.

Whatever bound his arms had broken, whether due to his strength or the fire it didn't matter, and allowed him to jump back up. Voices screamed around him from some invisible plain, but the fire died with their howls. He could see through the darkened space and the surprised faces of those in the foyer, but it didn't stop him from making his forward lunge towards McKinney.

The old man shouted as he retreated backwards. "Shoot him!"

A cacophony of shots rang out in the dark, overwhelming his senses. Men screamed around Archer, but he paid them no mind. He could do nothing but sprint towards his target. Nonetheless, not a single shot hit Archer.

This time McKinney jabbed the spear at Archer's throat. The flames tickled him. Archer clasped the blade in his neck and prevented it from piercing him further.

McKinney swore. "Why aren't you dead?"

"*It's my spear!*" Archer said. "*She gave it to me!*"

The burning man ripped the weapon from McKinney's hands, and the ache in Archer's chest quenched itself in an instant. The fire extinguished, and the newer blemishes on his skin and clothes vanished. It was as if the weapon had decided to cease harming him.

Archer pivoted with the spear and swiped at McKinney, slashing open his chest. Flames danced from the cut and sent the old geezer blazing to the floor. Gunshots fired, and Archer spun to meet them. He found that McKinney's men had either been downed or were engaged in a shootout between the pillars with what looked to be a giant of a man. Pure

82

mania erupted around the foyer with shots ricocheting off the pillars and walls.

McKinney didn't so much as scream but laugh as the fire tore through his flesh. Archer winced as the pyre swallowed everything before him.

A short vision of McKinney played in Archer's mind. A half-beaten man in a polo shirt and slacks was slumped in a corner of an empty office, clutching his broken fingers and sobbing. McKinney nodded to one of his men, and they fired into the skull of the unlucky sap. McKinney sighed in disappointment. He would have to get the cleaners in here again.

As quickly as the dream arrived, it departed. Archer was still in the mansion, as always.

The windows on the foyer's second floor creaked and shattered, sending glass across the open floor. A flood of crimson-stained darkness burst into the mansion. The living fog poured down and swallowed the burning McKinney, before bursting around the atrium as if a gas grenade had exploded under him. Whatever remained of his charred corpse could no longer be seen in the haze. Archer ran, and McKinney's men scattered from their firefight.

Archer darted around for an escape as the rest of the goons split up and poured out into the various mansion hallways. But was there any escape from this living death?

Charlie seized him by the shoulder. The big man pointed back to the hall that led to the basement. Archer didn't question him. There was no point.

The two dashed towards the kitchen. Men shouted in terror far behind the pair, and blood curdling shrieks soon followed. Archer looked back only once to where he had seen McKinney fall from the spear. In the mist, he thought he saw a lone flickering flame swimming in the miasma. It would only be a matter of time until it went out—or so Archer hoped.

Crimson wind whisked through the hallways. Visibility fogged further with every second they spent running. Charlie kicked open the basement door and shoved it closed behind them. Whistling wind whispered just outside the heavy wood. Puffs of red smoke pushed out from under the basement door. The duo tore off down the stairs.

The spear heated in Archer's hands. He ran the tip of the edge along the cavern walls from floor to ceiling and around the pathway in a circle. Fire sprouted out of the point and stained the cavern as it did earlier. He hoped it would also work as well to keep the encroaching darkness at bay as it did for the spiders earlier.

Slowly, the wave of mist ceased advancing. It halted by the fire and hovered uselessly like harbor fog over the water. Archer silently prayed that it would buy time for them to escape.

The two were wracked with hard breaths as they ran through the tunnel. They soon passed the flames from earlier that still burned on the cavern walls. However, the spiders had all disappeared. The big man wiped sweat from brow. Archer couldn't help but feel relief, too.

As the two ran on in silence, Archer couldn't ignore the elephant in the room any longer.

"How long have you been with Matilda?" he asked.

Charlie looked at him with hard eyes that softened for but an instant. He quickly turned away.

"I can guess. You admired her from afar. After being with her father as long as you have, I suppose it would make the most sense to avoid a situation where he would find out. We all know how that turned out."

The silent man nodded.

"Thank you for your help before. I know it was mainly for Matilda, but I'm still going to say it."

84

Charlie shrugged. Having a conversation was going to be impossible, but Archer needed to get a clue out of him. He must have known at least a little about this, especially since they were now looking for his girlfriend. There was no point asking now. All that would have to wait until they found her.

"Well, here's hoping she didn't stray too far off the path. She must have followed us down here for a reason."

Ahead, the tunnels that spun on in all directions were now all caked in white translucent wires and webbing that spread across every pathway forward. The spiders had not run: they were still here under the mansion, building base.

Down in the distance the slight clicking of thin legs could be heard tapping against stone. Archer counted hundreds of the pests up ahead.

Archer turned to Charlie, readying the red hot weapon in his hands. "I'm not going to be able to watch your back in there. Once this spear goes off, I can't just stop it."

The silent man nodded and gave a slight smile. He flexed an arm as if he were a strongman in an old circus show. Charlie clearly knew how to take care of himself.

Archer brought the spear down on the white strands, setting the wall of webs ablaze. Charlie checked his sidearm as the fire spread. While the white tangle burned, the pair pushed through the disintegrating strands and moved deeper into the tunnel towards the broken altar.

Matilda was waiting for them and, unlike with Ariane, he would be there this time. The whispering voice in his head wanted them all dead, but he wouldn't oblige it. Archer couldn't let the spear win.

"*Kill him! Kill him!*"

The anxiety bit at his nerves, but Archer ignored it and forced his beaten body through the tunnel. The spear continued demanding more of him. He couldn't let it get him now.

"Don't you desire me anymore, Christopher? Don't abandon me here!"

Cold fear washed over Archer. It took all he had to re-member that Ariane was dead and not coming back. The voice in his head wasn't real. She would never want others to die, especially not by his hands, and not her sister.

But then, who was this voice?

Charlie shook him by the shoulder. Archer had appar-ently been staring blandly at the ground as they ran. Archer slapped his own cheek.

"You're right," the spear-wielder said. "Everything else can wait: Matilda needs us. Lay on, MacDuff."

The pair disappeared into the dark, and now endlessly burning, tunnels. The spear told Archer that the enemy waited ahead, and it wanted their blood.

It made no difference what the spear or anyone else de-sired. Archer would push ahead regardless. No more stopping: it was time to burn these bastards to ash.

Chapter VIII
The Trap Collapses

"It's rather late," Ariane said.

The midnight hour shone through the hard snowfall of the winter season. The squall had covered him with the white powder, and there he stood at the doorway, brushing himself off. Christopher Archer had made his way here, despite the weather, and he was beginning to question if he was crazy for attempting this. He should be at home, safe in bed, and yet here he was at her place instead. This wasn't like him.

He looked upon his fiancé like he did every time he saw her. Her smile, her lithe figure in her blue nightgown, and her smooth steps towards him, made her seem like she walked out of a good dream. There she sat in her arm chair by the entrance to her apartment, watching as he fumbled for an excuse to explain why he was there. The truth was that he always had an excuse. Today, however, he was oddly nervous just looking at her.

"Christopher? What's wrong?"

"I wanted to give you this. It's your birthday tomorrow, after all." He handed her the small box he had hidden behind his back. "It's not that much, but you always tell me how you aren't wanting for much. I thought I'd put push that to the limit. Everybody needs something."

"Enigmatic as always. I can never tell what you're thinking."

"Says the girl with the fake her last name. Open it up. I would have gotten something better, but you can't get much for the girl who wants nothing."

Ariane knew he didn't have much. He never saw a need for anything. Christopher Archer moved from town to town since he left home at seventeen, mostly working odd jobs in places he came across. It was just enough to get by. What he never expected was a simple janitor job in a small town away from the bright lights of the city would give him what he never had. It was there that he would find Ariane Jones, a red-haired beauty with wit like a steel trap and a graceful poise that caught all the other guys' heads. She worked at the mayor's office, but she never said much to anyone outside of the job. Not until they met at the library.

Now he had someone, and he wasn't quite so sure what to do with her.

"A scarf?" She removed the small bundle of fabric from the box and wrapped it around her swan-like neck. It was the one with the light green and blue checkered pattern she had pointed out on one of their walks through the main street shopping area. Ariane giggled and winked a big blue eye at him as she cuddled up with the present. "Thank you! I didn't know I needed one."

"You don't wear enough for the weather. It's February, knucklehead. Do you want to catch a cold?"

She pressed the scarf tight to her neck. "Why don't you stay a while, Christopher? We can do some old puzzles I found at Aunt Cecilia's antique shop. Betty-Ann told me they're good ones."

"Much as I'd like to, I should go home. Reggie Wolverton's always wandering around late outside my place. Someone's gotta take him home, especially in this weather. Tomorrow, okay?"

"Tomorrow," she said, almost singing the words. "Only a few months until the big day. I can hardly wait."

He grinned, despite himself. "Me, too."

It took most of the energy he had to turn away from her, but he had to go. If he stayed any longer, there was no telling what he'd do, and what she'd let him get away with. Church early tomorrow morning meant he could at least find a better excuse to not give in to baser urges. Besides, he really did need to get back home. There was always tomorrow. He twisted the door knob when she spoke again.

"*It's too bad Reggie died in May, isn't it?*" Ariane said. "*I think he would have loved to attend the wedding.*"

A different sort of chill slipped down Archer's spine. He pivoted and found the apartment gone. Ariane had disappeared; and he was no longer in the past, but the crumbling existence that was the present. Only the cavern remained before him.

Archer was where he always was, shuffling through the dark tunnels with the big behemoth of Charlie by his side. The past intruding on his thoughts must have been a sign he was losing it. The spear was trying to take control. He tried to think of Matilda instead. She could still be saved—Ariane was long gone. Archer needed to remember that. It was all he could do to keep calm in this battleground between unreality and sanity.

The wide open altar awaited the two men, but it was left smashed to pieces. Spider webs had been strewn over the exposed area of the cavern where Archer had received his spear. The black ceiling over the altar remained pitch dark as if the top of it had been absorbed into the formless void.

A series of rough taps rapped from far above. Charlie

lightly stepped around the broken rubble that lay around the crater surrounding the altar, heading for the tunnel on the opposite side. Archer's ribs sparked with a jolt of pain. There was no telling how much more he could use this spear before his body gave in. He wasted no time following after Charlie.

They needed a way out of this place before the Eye consumed it all. Matilda was the only one left who might be able to aid them, if she could be found.

Ariane whispered in his ear. "*It was a perfect scarf, Christopher. Why did you leave? I wanted to give you a present of my own.*"

"You're not real," Archer said in a low voice. "You're dead."

"*The power pumping into your veins tells the truth. If you kill, we can be one. Don't run!*"

The last time Archer had seen Ariane alive was when they met at the coffee shop by Grant and Kenneth. His fiancé wore her hair up with a striking red ribbon to match her locks, and a light blue jacket to match the coming spring weather. Most times, they had met there when she was exhausted from a day of work. This time, she had picked out a puppy that caught her eye and wanted him to meet the little guy.

"You have to train them," he said. "Are we going to have time to do that with the wedding coming up? What's the runt going to do when we leave him alone for a few hours?"

"You worry too much, Christopher. Why do you let things you can't control get under your skin? I passed by the pet shop the other day, and I saw the look in his little eyes begging to be picked up. I can just imagine how he felt in that place with all those noisy cats, dirty hamsters, and disgusting spiders. It's just like the first time I saw you sitting in the library. You were asking someone to sit next to you."

"This story again. I told you, I just liked sitting alone.

It's relaxing. I'm no dog. Not everyone minding their business by themselves is begging to be rescued by Ariane Jones."

"No, just some." She smiled the last smile Christopher Archer had ever seen from her. "Guess what? When we get married, you're never going to be alone again. What do you say to that?"

He pretended to shiver. "Frightening."

"*Ha ha*. Let's visit him next week. You just know he's waiting for the right person to rescue him."

"There you go again. Not everyone is waiting to be rescued."

She pursed her lips and glanced out the window into the coming snow squall. "I think they are."

He had not understood what she meant at the time, but now that Archer could use these memories as a shield against the bitter thoughts assailing him, he was starting to. That is how he knew this voice wasn't his fiancé. She would never attack him like this. Ariane wasn't this presence.

Charlie reached the tunnel on the other end of the open space as Archer lagged behind. All that could be seen was the faint light of the torch on the altar and nothing else. The tapping in the emptiness above had shifted to subtle shuffling like a wave slipping up a beachhead. A hiss in the dark caused his palms to sweat against the spear shaft.

A glistening hairy, long-limbed spider-like body the size of a truck appeared for a brief instant before sinking back into the black shadows above. The cavern walls echoed with the tapping of rapid steps.

In the grim haze, a thick voice projected, booming across the empty void. "*For thousands of years, I had lain fallow in defeat due to the last mortal who wielded that spear. I bear you no grudge for the misfortune suffered upon me by that warrior. I will allow you a chance at life.*"

Charlie beckoned Archer to follow him into the tunnel, to ignore the voice, but Archer could only stare up into the emptiness. He waved Charlie to continue on without him.

Ariane shouted in his head again. "*Kill that beast, Christopher. It only wishes to tear us apart.*"

"Shut up, liar," he said in a low voice. Archer coughed before turning his attention back to the void. "I'm here for the girl! Where is she?"

"*Bearer of the spear, will you stand aside or be devoured?*"

"I don't stand aside for anyone. The Eye will be burned to ciders with the rest of this false world. Come down here and get a front row seat."

"*So be it.*"

A rattling hiss split the silence, and the stone cave rumbled. Archer tripped and stumbled over himself. Was that the monster hidden above, or yet another creature in this hell world?

The skittering form of a van-sized spider descended the tunnel wall. Its eight fur-covered legs stretched twice as long as a man's. The monster also held the build of a tarantula that had mated with an inbred Sasquatch. Its protruding jaw, barrel chest, and purplish red skin, couldn't have looked less human. Archer's mind went blank as he tried to understand just what he was looking at. When he realized this sight was actually real, the monster had already gotten within three meters of him. Archer lifted the spear in defense.

As he did so, the beast bounded sideways. Its large body slammed against the opposite side of the cavern. It leaped across the walls of the like a mad frog, cracking the rock base with its weight.

Charlie fired at it from the tunnel ahead of Archer. The bullet whistled past the spider's oblong head and bore into stone. The spider twisted around the shots and dove down on Archer, its jaws snapping.

The teeth closed on his neck, severing his skull from his spine—or it would have had he not kicked against its body. The sharp incisors slashed along Archer's cheek with its descent, snapping shut on the tip of his nose. Skin tore from his flesh and lime-colored blood trickled from the opening. Had he moved one second later, he would have lost his skull instead.

Charlie fired upon the spider as it sprang back. Three bullets sunk into its abdomen and purplish face, sending the beast to the floor. The oversized arachnid spun on its back, roaring madness before it flipped back to its long legs and tore past Archer towards Charlie, its greenish blood splashing everywhere.

Archer leaped after it. He sliced through the legs and the spider flipped to its belly. As it writhed, Archer jumped on top of the screeching beast. Its hissing brought the hairs on his neck up and a sinking feeling in his gut. He jabbed the spear down into the spider's skull. The arachnid's head burst open with the impact, leaking bright green tar blood everywhere.

The flame from the corpse swirled upwards along the strands and into the webs above. A chorus of shrieks erupted in the dark as it lit with the spear's fire like exploding stars in a demonic outer space. The entire cavern trembled as the flames burned. Stones and dislodged rock plummeted down from the lit webs above, slamming cinder block-sized hunks all over. At the same moment, hundreds of tiny voices hissed in the darkness over him.

"No time for this," Archer said. "Charlie, we're not gonna be alone for much longer. More of these things are coming!"

The two disappeared out the rear tunnel, following the slime trail the big man found. Charlie ran ahead, as if he had a destination in mind. Meanwhile, Archer perused the side tunnels. He scanned the walls, hoping for some hint as to where those spiders might have come out from. There, among the thick blankets of webbing inside a small crevice, he traced the outline of a figure enveloped in the white strands. Archer ran his fingers along the substance, searching for a loose end to pry.

Cries roared from the tunnels behind him like thunder from heaven. They wouldn't be distracted by the fire forever.

Archer pushed at the webbing, using the spear to saw through the gunk. Trickles of flame tore up the strands. As the webbing pulled apart, a man fell out of it. Archer caught Miles in his arms. The whimpering man's legs were crooked and noticeably thin under his pant legs.

"You came back?" Miles asked.

"Not by choice. There's nowhere else to go. You'll see."

The inhuman cries howled louder as the ground quaked yet again. Archer dodged a rock the size of a basketball dropping from the ceiling. It embedded itself into the earth.

"They're going to be here soon," Miles said. He coughed a spurt of that familiar alien green liquid from his lips. "You better find your way out quick."

"You're bleeding."

"So are you. The spider bites don't heal. My clothes keep repairing themselves, but not my skin. I don't know where these freaks came from, but they weren't here before we came down."

"They're part of the Eye. It attacked once it realized the spear was free. The spiders want to turn us into entrées before it can get to the main course. With the spear out of the way, it'll get to Earth."

Blood dribbled down Miles' lips. "We really stepped in it by coming here."

"They're manifestations from nightmares. I thought

94

they would have died when their creator did." Archer ignored the doubt that sprang into his head. McKinney *had* to be dead. The Eye must have gotten his remains by now, if there was anything left. "We have to get out before the spiders return."

"Your theory has teeth, like those things. They took a bite out of me, remember? I can't walk."

"How does that matter?" A dislodged boulder shattered in the center of the tunnel behind him. "I guess I gotta carry you out. Grab hold."

"Don't be ridiculous, Christopher." His breaths choked into a moan. Bright neon liquid seeped through the suit material. "I think that webbing held my insides together, because it's really kicking in now."

"This place won't let you die, Miles."

Miles ejected a stream of green blood from his mouth, and his Caucasian skin whitened to a hard pale shade. He shivered. "I'm j-just lucky. I g-get o-out of here b-before you."

"McKinney screwed everyone. All these damn things want us dead from every angle. Get up, Miles."

"The o-only thing they fear is the s-spear. Don't give it to them, C-Christopher."

A mad joy at the notion of killing more of these things danced inside Christopher Archer's heart. More blood, more carnage. He fought off the smile sneaking onto his lips. "Miles?"

"Look out for the big guy. He's too dumb to be left on his own. Just watch. *Him.*"

With those words, Miles stilled, and his tongue stiffened. He rolled over onto his back in a lifeless lump and did not move again .All that remained of Miles was a bleeding corpse.

Archer stood up in time for a flood of boulders to rain down upon the pair. He fled as a pile bashed against the cavern floor. Hisses screeched out of the tunnels again. Hundreds of tiny bodies scampered across the walls down the pathways. The earth quaked and threw him off balance, but still he managed to sprint towards the back tunnel.

The thunderous clattering of thousands of small taps made him look back but once. The darkness filled with tiny purple bodies each with eight scampering legs. The fires from the burnt webbing had lit some of the bastards ablaze as they gave chase, burning them to cinders.

As he twisted down the thin tunnels, the ceiling rained down rocks onto the path. The stones batted against him, knocking Archer about in his run. A boulder dashed his skull, causing his right eye to throb. But he couldn't stop moving forward. Getting trapped by rubble, or caught by those fat sack arachnids, would be the end. Archer swerved around the falling debris.

He couldn't see any more spiders behind him, partially because the path filled with falling rocks blocking the way backwards. Instead he focused on the road ahead. The quakes didn't cease, but at least he could escape the spiders' pursuit, for now.

Through the trembling stone a constant hammering matched it in tempo. Archer followed the beating cacophony with the spear burning in his grip.

At the end of the short path, he found Charlie kneeling in front of a narrow vertical crevice. The large man hammered at the rocks with the butt of his gun. Matilda stood on the other end of the stone from Charlie and watched the giant pry open the rocks blocking her in.

"What are you two doing?" Archer said. "The tunnel is falling apart!"

"Christopher?" Matilda asked. "Is that you? I was running from the spiders and got trapped in here when I tried to hide. Charlie, you two should get out now."

Charlie shook his head, and Archer sighed.

"Hold still, Matilda. We'll get you out. Move over, Charlie."

Archer joined Charlie in striking the stone. The spear's blade slashed through the opening quite well. Whatever it had been forged out of must have been a durable material since it took several strikes to break a space for her to slide out of. Charlie leaned through to grab her and took the woman up into his arms. Archer led them both back out into the tunnels.

Yet more quakes brought more boulders to bear down on them. A giant rock bashed against Charlie's right arm, causing him to stagger. Archer turned in time to get cracked across the jaw with stone and weaved sideways. The tremors only increased, making it hard to hear anything but the downpour of boulders.

Archer shouted back, and Charlie charged ahead to meet his pace. The giant was barrelling onward with purpose, and the girl. Archer couldn't help feel some envy, but it wouldn't matter if they were dead.

Light broke through the opening ahead in a slightly muted tinge of red. A jagged rock slashed across Archer's arm, choking off a grunt. Stones beat across them with every step, but still they moved onward. Stones slammed against him even as he tore towards the exit.

Twenty feet and they'd be free. The two rushed through the opening in time for the walls and ceiling to come down. Matilda shouted, and Charlie leaned over her to avoid the stones crushing his head or striking her. The big man grimaced but plowed forward regardless. Only ten feet to go!

Archer slashed at the falling stones, and the duo darted out of the darkness into the red mist. The shower of boulders crashed down behind them. The rubble sealed the path with a cavalcade of slamming stone. Charlie and Archer lost their footing and tripped to the pile of rocks and dirt.

They both took heavy breaths and wiped the sweat from their brow. Archer stood first and shook himself free of dirt. Matilda, still in Charlie's hold, looked up at her man mystified.

"I told you to leave. Why did you come back for me, Charlie?"

Archer answered for him. "Why wouldn't he?"

"Because it's my fault he's like this. Papa caught him trying to take me away. He said he wouldn't have another child disobey him. It's my fault Ariane is—"

Charlie put his fingers on her lips and shook his head. Archer could somehow understand just what he meant. The big man pointed his thumb back at the chaos of crumbled stone.

"It was your father," Archer said. "Not you. Not even Miles knew what was going on."

"That ceremony exists for sacrificing the one you love the most. I heard him say it, even if I didn't believe him when he said it. If my father would have preferred me more than her . . . she would still be alive. I couldn't do anything to save my sister. I couldn't even save Charlie."

"That doesn't appear to bother him."

Charlie sat beside her in the dirt and shrugged. Archer remembered what Miles had said about this guy before. He had a one track mind, but nobody knew just what for or why. It probably wouldn't be any easier to understand him even if he could speak. Charlie checked Matilda's wounds over, but they had already healed over. She had no spider bites, unlike him.

She shrunk away from him, shielding her eyes from his bleeding bites. "Charlie is Charlie."

"You two been an item long?"

She blushed and glared at Archer. "That's none of your business. Instead, tell me where those spiders came from. What are they?"

He told her briefly about the mausoleum before pointing to the dark red mist peaking over the edge of the hill before them. "We should get to higher ground. Those spiders might come back."

This was not the proper exit of the cavern. It was merely a space where the ceiling had already caved in long before they got there. Walls of sheer cliff encircled them with only the slant of rubble ahead to guide them back out to the surface. The hard red tint of the sky had deepened since the last time he had seen the outside.

Archer pushed forward up the steep pile of stone, and his footing wobbled with his climb. There was too much rubble for just the spear to have caused this. The forest and the mansion had to have been consumed by the Eye by now. Was any of this world left up there on the surface?

He reached the top of the hill and the thick crimson fog. The space where the woods would be had completely masked itself in the red void. Archer turned around to face the mansion and was not too surprised to find it completely missing.

But what replaced it caused a cold feeling to buckle his knees.

Instead of the mansion, the halls and rooms of the large house had been dashed about the endless open space in some mockery of a maze across the flat plain. A new black sky dotted with red stars bore down on them. The new moon reminded him of an eyeball. This eye stared down on the labyrinth as if watching the mice stumble about inside its experiment. As Archer stared up into the flashing pupil, the red mist around the maze slowly dissipated. The spear at his side shook violently.

The Eye!

He thought he heard distant screams on the wind, but they came and left as if blown by in the breeze. In the cascade he thought he heard *her*.

"*I'm waiting.*"

No longer did he care if they used *her* voice to trick him. Even if it made his fists clench involuntarily, it didn't bother him to hear her anymore. She was waiting for him.

All he had to do was destroy the Eye. The spear would let him do it.

Archer made his way towards the mansion maze, his blackened skin burning with his ribs. Matilda called out from behind him, but he put no stock in her presence. More important tasks lay ahead of Christopher Archer. His blood boiled with the knowledge that there was more violence to come. The spear was ecstatic, and it would be fed what it needed to do the job ahead.

Out in the dark, a beast howled for death. This world wasn't quite dead yet, just as he wasn't.

"I hear you, Ariane. The blood is coming."

Chapter IX
Blood Maze

Footsteps shuffled behind Archer as he marched from the remains of the forest towards the newly emerged labyrinth. He had no time to stop for anyone else, not when Ariane was waiting for him.

Only harsh streaks of poisonous red sunlight from the Eye shone down on the maze where the house had once stood. Now, instead of that gargantuan mansion, he looked upon the set of obscure hallways strewn about seemingly at random that spun all about in strange directions with balding pine trees dotting the impossible space between the rows. The roof had vanished, but he could recognize pieces of that oversized mansion anywhere. He had the impression that the universe had reassembled the matter of the house and regurgitated it into a mess of hallways with jagged turns for what went on for miles into the dark of this limbo. Voices screeched somewhere in that mess. Had there been anything left unconsumed by the Eye?

Matilda gasped from behind him. "Papa actually did it."

Archer didn't turn around, nor did he care about McKinney anymore. There was still more blood to consume somewhere nearby. He approached the wall blocking his entrance into the mansion maze with the two sets of footsteps still trailing after him. Menace wafted off of the broken boards and torn insulation that stuck out of the reassembled surface.

"He's still in there," Archer said. "The spear knows—it needs more of his blood, his heart. It wants him whole."

"The spear talks to you?" Matilda asked.

"Oh, I forgot you weren't there," Archer said without turning around. He slashed apart the wall, sending the pieces flying in cinders. "I'm now one with the spear. It's part of the deal."

"*Tell her about me*," Ariane said.

"Shut up."

"What is it telling you, Christopher?" Matilda whispered behind him.

"To kill." He turned back to meet the two of them. Both Matilda and Charlie stared at him as if he were about to pass out. His insides broiled under his charred skin, causing untold aching, but he wouldn't let them know that. "The spear tastes flesh nearby, so it's going to eat it. You shouldn't follow me."

"Where else are we going to go?" Matilda asked. "The Eye is going to get us all. My father summoned that monster, but I bet he didn't expect it to do this much. He wanted to become one with this thing, but just look up at that disgusting creature up there! It whispers when you even take a glance at it."

"Your father isn't a stupid man. He learned about the spear; he learned about the Eye; and he brought us all to this place because he knew a way to get both. There is a one in a billion chance that if there's a single person who knows how to walk out of this in one piece I would bet everything that it's Joseph McKinney."

Charlie lifted up a hand for silence. The big man

searched around, scanning the dead ground.

"You hear something, do you?" Archer said. "It's your choice if you want to come with me. Don't get mad if whatever is in there drags you down to hell."

"Be careful, Charlie," Matilda said. "The Eye wants us all."

Charlie kissed her on the cheek, and she flinched. A surge of anger flooded through Archer for a reason he couldn't understand and didn't care to. She followed behind Charlie and in front of Archer as they moved. The spear-wielder watched the rear.

Inside the labyrinth, the former mansion floorboards had melted into the grass, leaving an odd mismatched pattern of green and brown across the black blades. Lush leaves and branches hugged the wallpaper and dipped dead brush upon the torn carpeting. The red mist rolling in brought a stench of garbage to the forlorn atmosphere. The Eye hanging above appeared to follow their movements, but Archer couldn't be certain due to its Sun-like size.

Charlie led the three through the mist. As they moved, Archer heard what the big man was getting agitated about earlier. A familiar voice shouted nearby, not too far from their position.

Several hallways repeated themselves in twist and turns. Archer ran a hand across the surface of the walls and found mud smearing his fingertips. But the muck stunk of a pungent rank worse than old banana peels and curdled milk. The picture frames, wooden beams, and carpets, were all constructed of this same material.

Archer slashed open the nearby door, and liquid splashed out from what he thought was solid. The faux material disintegrated into nothing at his feet. Archer moved into the opening and found an obscure room constructed of patchwork boards and wallpaper. In the center of the floor, a hole had been dug.

The three peered down into the pit. Doyle twisted and shouted in agony at the bottom of the hole. The maniac was splotched with green liquid and was surrounded by dead spider bodies. Mad laughs escaped from him when he realized he was being watched.

"You can't eat spiders!" Doyle said. "But you can step on them."

"McKinney left you down there?"

"The fog made it hard to breathe; but then the ground crumbled, and the air changed. It was amazing, Archer! Then these *things* came out of the earth and tried to eat me. *Me!* Can you just imagine? I never knew Mr. McKinney was so powerful."

Archer tried not to let his disdain for this fool show. "McKinney left you down there. Show us how to get to him. You have no loyalty to the bastard. He abandoned you here to die."

"You know it, Archer. The only ones who know it are myself, Len, and a few others. Too bad Len's dead, and the others were already eaten. They've ascended! Did you know that?"

Matilda answered instead. "I didn't."

"You wouldn't, Princess," Doyle said. His grin stained with green teeth flickered to bitter rage. "I can hear them coming. It is our turn to join him."

"Great, Doyle's lost it." Before Archer could continue, he spotted Charlie furrowing his brow at the man in the pit. He looked to be puzzling a thought out. "What is it, Charlie? Is he lying?"

"Look, Christopher!" Matilda gestured to the pit. The earth quaked, and stone shifted under Doyle's bloodstained boots. "The ground is moving."

"As well it should," Doyle said. "It is time for my reward. You all better pray he is as gracious with you."

The dirt in the pit melted and twisted upwards out of its solid form like a viper. It snapped at Doyle, embracing him in its tight grip. He shivered as the purplish-black tsunami encircled and swallowed him down into its makeshift mouth. Every trace of what Doyle had once been was lost to the substance. The pit filled itself in not unlike a sandpit covering over itself. Doyle had been eaten by the very world itself.

Red mist crawled across the flat ground, drifting about where the former pit had once been. A crash brought the three survivors to attention. Strange whispers bit at Archer's ears through the still air.

"What happened to him?" Matilda asked. "It ate the spiders, too?"

Archer put up a hand. "Quiet!"

It took an additional moment for him to figure out the whisper wasn't speaking from the spear again. The speech on the air slowly lowered from a murmur into a booming voice on the building breeze. The laughing tone of Doyle filled the space.

"*All three of them are here, sir!*"

Wood split and crunched behind the trio. Six giant figures broke open the wall into the makeshift room. Charlie flinched as he saw what they were and put Matilda behind him.

A squadron black suits of armor stared the three of them down, wobbling clumsily forward. Archer hardly recognized them as the ones from the mansion, covered in the dirt of this world. The six puppets converged on their prey with jerking movements. Their swords whistled as they were brought up and then down again.

Charlie pushed the girl to the dirt and the blade whistled over her head. The big man charged the attacking suit of steel, pushing it back along the grass not unlike a gored bullfighter. The armor squeaked, and the two fighters fell over into the muck.

The five other suits moved in, swords and shields brandished. Archer struck one of the armor automatons and sparks burst from its plating. The fire burned, but barely left a stain. A sword bit his cheek. Trickles of green blood ran down his skin. What were these things made of?

Numbness ran through his wound. They might not have been made of steel or mud, but what they were made of was enough to plow through the likes of him. If they weren't so clumsy, these puppets would be more of a threat.

"*Charlie!*" Matilda shouted.

Behind Archer, the ground swirled up and covered the girl. She sank down into the earth like quicksand, just as Doyle had. The remaining armored suits encircled Archer, preventing him from giving aid. Charlie dove into the dirt towards his girlfriend.

She slipped through the earth and out of view as Charlie reached for her. He dug his meaty fingers into the mud and began frantically digging. The ground trembled again as the big man madly pushed downwards. Archer tried to shout for him, but the giant wasn't listening. He didn't see the armor behind him lifting its sword to strike.

"Behind you, Charlie!" Arched yelled.

One of the armored men ran Charlie through with his sword. He jerked and spat as he went limp, green blood dribbling on his lips before he stilled on the ground. Four of the armors dove on top of his corpse. They morphed into the same dark mud substance and sunk down with their prisoner into the dirt, just as Matilda had moments ago. Soon all that was left was Christopher Archer to face the lone remaining armor by himself. He kept away from the muddy areas to avoid a similar fate to his companions. The suit still burned as it encroached on him.

The enemy swung its blade at Archer in a shower of strikes. He deflected each hit, his arms trembling with the attacks.

"*I told you not to bet against Mr. McKinney,*" the armor said. "*Now you're going to be nothing but a babbling lobotomy patient in a cell, wishing for death. But it will never come.*"

"Very impressive, Doyle." Archer used the moment to take a breath. "You're not dead."

"*None of us can die here, Archer. How do you not understand this yet? You're simply one of the weaker pieces the knights and rooks knock over before they reach the end of the board.*"

"What about Len?" Archer asked. "He's dead."

"*Your spear stole him first. It doesn't matter. Once we consume you, we will get him back. All will be one with the Eye.*"

"Matilda, Charlie, Miles, your friends, McKinney, you . . . it took you all. It's not on your side, and still you gloat?"

A fierce earthquake growled. Both Archer and the armor suit lost their balance and fell against the weak walls. The tremors harshened with each passing second.

"*We're all here. Those two lovebirds are struggling, but soon they'll join us, too. It is all as inevitable as death in the old world. Though I suppose there is no more death for us, is there?*"

When Archer felt tempted to look up at the Eye, a sensation in his arm stopped him. The spear was speaking to him. As he felt for his weapon, the armor attacked. The sword slashed for his throat, and Archer guarded. He slid backwards on the black grass, his fingers stinging in the grip of his spear.

He struck it again, and the flames gushed out, flowing across the armor. The suit danced about, attempting to put the fire out. Archer used the chance to run past his enemy.

He sprinted down the rumbling path of warped mansion walls. It would take time for the armor to catch up. The breather at least gave him a chance to think as he ran around the maze's sharp corners.

Even with the obviously fake halls and floors made of that black tar, he was treated to more disturbing sights that caused his skin to sweat and pale. Illness punched at his gut. In his dash, he caught the sight of dead men everywhere.

Stiff limbs and eyeless heads stuck out of the ground throughout the maze. They peeked out awkwardly like statues that had let growth overtake them over the centuries; some were full corpses, but most were only body parts jutting out from the dead earth. None bled or showed signs of injury, but all decorated the maze as an obscure horror show.

The corpses were all a part of this world, like they were decorations no different than the trees or the dilapidated paintings on these false mansion walls.

Even worse was that there were dozens of them. He recognized several as the same men Archer had met guarding this very mansion. McKinney had built a mausoleum for his own conquests, of his pleasant memories. Their bodies were nothing but trophies for him, if they were even real anymore.

"Why are you running, Christopher?"

A new white hot rage burned inside Archer. That voice wanted in his head again. "Stop it. You're not her."

"Just kill them all."

"Why can't you leave me alone? They're all already dead. Until I find McKinney, nothing is stopping the geezer from bringing them back from the dead again and again."

He hopped over an obscure arm sticking from the

ground. He could have sworn the fingers moved, but refused to stop and confirm.

"I have enough on my plate without you in my head," Archer continued.

"*Are you satisfied with allowing The Eye to kill more?*"

"I haven't been satisfied since she died. You using her voice doesn't make me want to do your bidding. It's making me want to break you in two and toss you to the wind with the rest of the madmen. Whatever demon made you is a monster beyond my comprehension."

"*You still don't believe me. So be it.*"

The sudden heat in the spear spiked, sending smoke up from his aching palms. He had to let it go, even though there was nothing he wanted less. The weapon struck the ground, and a harsh white light pitched out the shining edge and bored into his brain like a drill. Archer buckled and shielded his eyes. Had the spear melted?

When he opened his eyes—a woman stood before him where the spear had fallen. Familiar golden red hair flowed from her head and soft white skin adorned her naked body. Ariane, with her curved hips and plentiful bosom more noticeable than ever in this dark world, watched him intently. She stayed as he remembered her, except for one thing. Those hard, mean eyes stuck out as utterly alien to the fiancé he knew.

The poisonous smile dawning on her perfect soft lips as her slender arms folded under her breasts was unlike any he had ever seen from her before. But she breathed, she moved, and she spoke, just as Ariane did.

"With the amount of blood you devoured," she said, "I can now walk free."

Archer bit his lip involuntarily. A frenzy of uncontrollable urges built up in him. "Stay back!"

"Don't be like that. It's me, Christopher. I've seen

things, experienced ecstasy you will never believe. That is, until you also see it. Join me in the spear, in the blood, where we can be together again. The more blood, the more life we consume, the longer we can be together. Unleash the flames—swallow everything into you."

His skin crawled and twisted with every word she spoke. It was her voice, and it *was* her. Ariane had been returned to him. But she was missing a vital piece that made her who she was.

He ran his palm across her cheek, and she clasped it with both hands. They were as small as he remembered, though considerably hotter. Ariane kissed his knuckle and smiled up at him. A single set of tears ran down both her cheeks.

"I can hold you again," she said.

Archer embraced her, squeezing hard. She returned the favor. Ripples of joy washed through him as he gripped her soft, supple body and smelled her sweet fragrance once again. This heat was the missing chasm in his being he had gone without for so long. He would never let her go again.

"They took me from you; they took you from me, Christopher." Her voice warbled, and she paused with her face in his chest. She choked back tears. "*They're all going to die for it.*"

He took a breath, his eyes closed. His voice choked in his throat. "That's what you want me to do?"

"There's nothing left here that isn't less than a beast. They've all chosen the Eye. There is no saving them. They're worms wriggling scorched earth. We are all that is left."

"They aren't all worms."

"How can you say that after all they've done? After everything they've taken from you?"

Christopher Archer held Ariane McKinney by the

shoulders. She looked up to him with a blazing fire that could melt hell itself. Her hard gaze locked with his. He couldn't stomach what she was saying. "Matilda and Charlie did what they could to save me. Miles didn't deserve what happened to him. They aren't all like Len or Doyle . . . or your father."

"They all let me die. Every one of them."

"They didn't know what your father was planning. They didn't know what he would do to you."

"*The hell they didn't!*" Her teeth bared, she pushed back at Archer despite his tight hold. Her surprising strength bruised his already scarred chest, but still he wouldn't let her go. "It burns. It always burns. It never stops hurting. They all *need* to feel it like I have to. Why can't you see, Christopher? You have to understand it. They took me away from you!"

Tremors interrupted her words. The earthquake knocked them about, but still they refused to budge from each other's grip. Archer bit his lip as his fiancé raged on in his arms. Sooner or later, McKinney would attack them again. Ariane had to wake up before that happened.

"I understand it, Ariane. You know I do. But if it wasn't for your sister and her man, I never would have found you. We wouldn't be together again."

"Do you think I can just forgive them? After all I've been through, after the flames still refuse to melt my very being?" Tears welled in her burning gaze. "I can't do it. Not even for you!"

"Then hold that rage, for now. We all have a common enemy. As long as he's alive, there's still the Eye to worry about. And what if it leaves this place and returns to Earth? Can you live with turning home into this place?"

"Why should I care? None of them cared when they did this to me. I want it all scorched to cinders. It can all burn!"

"You don't mean that."

Choking sobs wracked her speech. Archer lifted her small chin with a finger and watched as her wrath momentarily cooled.

"I have to," she said.

Archer squeezed her tight as a bang erupted from the maze. Somewhere nearby the clanking of armor had struck the artificial walls. Doyle's suit of armor was catching up to them. "Don't worry, Ariane. They're never going to hurt you again."

Ariane nodded in his hold, and a flash of light erupted from her body. Once more he was blinded. When he opened his eyes, she was gone, and the spear was in his grip once more.

"*Found you, Archer!*"

The suit of armor slashed through the wall behind him, and Archer fell upon the enemy. With a guttural cry, he tore into it.

The spear refused to break the armor, but he weaved around the sword strikes and cleaved into it with an anger he had never felt before. A new rage took hold of him that was completely separate from the spear. This fresh energy pumped through his muscles with something more potent than blood—pure vitriol. The weapon pierced the walking armor, splitting it in two. Doyle's voice screamed from inside the suit, which gave away to the loudest and harshest laugh that Archer was capable of producing. The sliced armor didn't fall, it instead lunged forward.

Doyle's sword pierced Archer's stomach, and he winced. The earthquake rang out again with a fury unlike any this world had seen before, causing the mansion walls to completely crumble. Archer didn't have time to notice it as his gut flared with agony.

"*I've got you, Archer,*" Doyle said. "*Once I have that spear, Mr. McKinney is going to—*"

Archer slashed the helmet, smashing it apart with a single cut. A bonfire erupted inside the suit. Archer diced it again and again until nothing was left but scrap. With every cut, Doyle screamed like a butchered pig. But Archer refused to stop until the fires finally ate it whole. Doyle's anguished cries evaporated as if it were sucked into the atmosphere. The armor melted into the soil as Doyle was taken to whatever hell awaited him.

Archer threw the sword from his gut. "McKinney isn't going to do anything but burn."

Before he could sense it, another suit of armor slipped upwards through the dirt like reverse quicksand. Its sword descended on Archer's skull but missed, instead digging into his shoulder. He ducked backwards, but the armor wouldn't cease its flurry of attacks.

His skin was slashed open, but still Archer struck back. No matter how many times these things would try to finish him off, he told himself he would hit back three times as hard. The armor pierced his heart, sending that familiar neon green blood from his bellowing mouth, but still he attacked. The spear sliced the enemy down the center. Useless metal, or whatever it was supposed to be, scattered over the uneven earth. He stared up at the Eye.

"*Christopher!*" Ariane said.

"We can't die here," he said, fully knowing it was no longer true. "Remember?"

"*You're bleeding.*"

He looked down at his wounds, and the ground below him split. The entire universe underneath Archer cracked in two, splitting at the seams.

"*This world is unstable. You don't have much time left. Please, just . . .*"

Her words froze in his mind as if she caught herself saying the wrong thing. Whatever she wanted to tell him was canceled out by whatever she wanted him to do. This weapon had a hold on her, perhaps even tighter than it had on him, but he still had one thing left to do before either the spear or the Eye swallowed them all whole.

"Ariane, you—"

But the world beneath his feet gave away. Stone and earth, or its closest facsimile in this place, gave way to nothing as trees and the false maze crumbled into dust in the non-existent air. The remaining red mist swirled away in a tornado of oblivion, taking away the ground and the sky with it.

Soon enough, the Eye had vanished, and Archer was left alone with his spear, dying alone in the darkness.

Even as he choked on the vacuum of the void, he kept the weapon close to his chest. There was a man that had to die, and Archer would see it through to the end, even if it tore him to pieces. With Ariane by his side, he could do anything. Death could wait for the vengeance that needed to be delivered on Joseph McKinney.

For the second time since killing Doyle, Archer laughed a maniac's laugh in the voiceless void. The last of his patience and humanity had scorched away, leaving him with nothing but the drive to kill. She was waiting for him. All he was left with in the dark were his last sparks of hate, and the spear.

The time for flames was at hand, and he was their agent.

CHAPTER X
Death on the Moon

"I'm always here, Christopher."

"I know."

Christopher Archer awoke to the grip of sub-zero ice crushing in on his organs. The darkness swirled and choked his breaths from his lungs. He still held the spear despite the rest of him aching with open cuts and unhealed burns. Green blood pumped out of him, but his energy and focus remained intact. He couldn't lose now. The weapon gave him all the motivation he needed to move.

"Kill him! Kill him!"

In mere moments, Archer would do just that. Just as soon as he saw something other than a black pit of nothing surrounding his prone form. Archer furrowed his brow as a migraine ripped through his woozy skull. Harsh light slowly brightened before his scrunched eyes.

A volley of stars broke through the black, watching over him from their perch in space. Hard stone suddenly solidified under his back. He sat up with a groan. The white rock underneath him stretched on into the curved horizon. He was no longer on Earth, or whatever facsimile of Earth this limbo was supposed to be.

Over the round white horizon, a giant sphere drifted far in the distance: a planet. The red clouds and dark waters would have made him guess it an alien world: but the geography of continents clearly marked it as Earth's. If it wasn't for the black seas and glimmering rouge-colored clouds he might think it was home, but it did give him context for where he was standing.

Archer was on the moon. And he was alive.

"But I can breathe," he said.

"Because it's not the moon. It's the last remnant of my world before the Eye consumes it whole."

Over his shoulder, Archer spotted McKinney. The old geezer stepped across the moon itself, hands behind his back. Plumes of dust kicked up under his slow steps, and yet he moved at a quick speed incongruous with what Archer was seeing. The old man blitzed across the surface, stopping several dozen feet before him. McKinney's expression never wavered from its dead glare.

Behind the old man, a blurry mass of dark red vines slipped out of an invisible curtain of nothingness. The abyss of space itself cracked, allowing Archer to see the tendrils connected to the old man. They moved like puppet strings behind McKinney.

Ropes of thick rouge-colored tendrils stuck out of McKinney's back, stretching back into the distance and into the fractured sky above. As Archer traced their barely visible presence, he caught a glimpse of a whole new planet hovering where the sun should be. But it wasn't a planet at all, it was an eye.

The impossible flaming eyeball had a slit pupil like a beast, its wires attached to McKinney from a distance of easily over a hundred million kilometers. It blinked when the old man did, but the burning red sphere never ceased casting putrid crimson light upon the false universe. They were one being now.

The geezer yawned at Archer. McKinney had accomplished his goal, yet he didn't appear to care what it had cost him to reach it.

"Once you hand over my spear, we can finally get on with this."

"The spear drains your life, McKinney. I'm barely holding together as it is." While that was the truth, Archer's concern rested more with Ariane. She had clearly reached a tipping point, judging from her demeanor, and one more douse of death from a kill might be the push she needs to be lost forever inside the spear. McKinney would not understand it—he could never understand how his daughter suffered. "The reason the wielders never live long is because it takes their life force. Being one with this Eye isn't going to change that for you."

"Don't play the idiot with me, rodent. The Eye sees through whatever it touches: it's what allowed it to pierce through this purgatory I created. That spear, once tamed, will be no different. I will never suffer from its inconveniences."

"But I know someone who will."

"Who?" McKinney asked. "That spear is eating you? So what. As if I care about the man who murdered my daughter. Give it to me and you can be spared from its effects. I can solve everything if you would just get out of the damn way!"

"That's rich, McKinney. Didn't you just murder Matilda? You're hardly one to lecture."

"Look here." McKinney pointed to an empty space to the left of Archer. The non-existent air rippled, and the invisible atmosphere split open to reveal a scene playing out in a black pit. Inside, Matilda and Charlie were surrounded by a dozen or so half-rotten purple bodies beating at the two as if trying to tear them apart. Bruises and welts covered both, and still Charlie attempted to shield the woman. McKinney rolled his eyes. "They are being punished, but when purified, they will join me. Only you will taste oblivion when I am finished with your trivial existence."

Archer's sore fingers tightened around his spear. "I'm not concerned about me. It's Ariane you should care about. She is the one who you're hurting more than anyone."

"I'm not going to warn you again about saying her name. I see everything, Archer. The Eye shows me all."

Clearly that was false, but Archer had little way of proving it without revealing his only play left. He concentrated on the spear, and tried to reach Ariane again. Deep down his thoughts whispered into the charred void of his soul. Pressure in his brain released like a loosened clamp and a warm sensation flooded inside. Tiny whispers touched his mind and rolled to his lips.

She wanted to speak, so very badly. Archer knew he shouldn't let her—not when she was so far gone from who she once was—but McKinney needed to know what he was doing. He needed to understand just what madness he had let loose on his own family.

Archer's lips moved without him speaking. "*When you dragged me down there, did you even think about what Mama would have thought?*"

Hard shivers trickled across Archer's skin. That wasn't his voice coming out of his mouth. But the warmth forming in the depths of his marrow made it all okay. Ariane was pushing through him, and he let her do it.

"That can't be," McKinney said. "Why are you speaking through *him*?"

"*Don't answer me with questions*," Ariane said. Her voice roared from Archer's mouth as if shouted from a bullhorn. "*I wasn't the first. You killed Mama, didn't you?*"

"She was already on death's door, Ariane. Your mama would do anything to help me, but she lost her life studying that spear. She died so that I could grow beyond life. Perhaps she's with you now."

"*No one is in here but the tormented and unending wails of the undying. You've destroyed so much, Papa. Now you will meet the Reaper for it.*"

"Once I take you from there, and *him*, we can be a family again. The two of us, and Matilda."

"*Bring her here!*"

"Of course!"

McKinney twisted his wrist and squeezed his fist in a dramatic gesture. Both Matilda and Charlie tumbled from the portal and landed on the moon's surface in the space between Archer and McKinney. Charlie's breaths fell heavy as green blood dripped from his wide open gashes. He lay there writhing next to Matilda. The woman stood up between the possessed Archer and her father, watching both parties intently. McKinney raised both hands in triumph as the portal closed once more.

"See, Ariane? I didn't lose anything. You're both still here, and everyone who opposed me has been wiped away into atoms. The immortality you have been granted is because of me. Why are you so upset about my gift? Matilda has always been the ungrateful one. Not you."

"*I'm always on fire because of you,*" Ariane said. "*I see nothing but scorched bones and cooked viscera every moment of my existence, and I can never escape it. Never. It's because of you.*"

"But you can't die, can you? Very short-sighted, dear. You will learn to love it."

"*Kill them all, Christopher!*"

Both McKinney and Matilda blanched at the vicious tone of her voice. But Archer would follow her instructions. She knew what to do, and he had nothing else but her presence to keep him warm. This lot would pay for what they had done.

Archer couldn't hold back the wild grin spreading across his face. So much gore for the spear—for *her*. She would have it all. Her revenge would wipe the last trace of this scumbag family from existence—and then they could take it back to Earth. There were so many men who deserved to be impaled, screaming for mercy as their blood drained and their flesh charred. All that potential chaos to be used on the unclean allowed his hunger to grow. First, it would start with Joseph McKinney.

The old man only sighed and shrugged at her words. "I see you're still nothing but a spoiled girl. You and your dog can't kill me here. This is my world. You're my daughter, not an oaf's plaything. We have bigger plans ahead of us. Give me my spear."

"*He will give you the spear, and you will give him your guts as they spill out into this false moon before your tainted soul is consumed by hellfire.*"

"That's more than enough out of you. I'll be waiting in the Eye, Ariane. When you've finally calmed and accepted your new reality, I will take you back. Until then, you can do what you want with the trash and your sister. But I know you will never hurt family. It's all you've ever had."

McKinney drifted up above the moon as if caught in a heavy gust and soared away. He flew towards the giant Eye, the red tendrils folding into him as he shot through space. Soon, he disappeared from sight, leaving the party of three—four including the voice in Archer's head—standing alone on the false moon. But the rage at the center of Archer's thoughts did not cool even slightly.

He looked upon the visibly-trembling Matilda. She ducked down, shielding the wounded Charlie, as if expecting Archer to run him through. The woman had good instincts—Archer was readying himself to do just that.

"Please don't kill him, Ariane," Matilda said to Archer.

"*What makes you believe you have any say over my decisions, bitch?*"

Tears streamed down Matilda's dirty cheeks. "I'm sorry I didn't catch on until it was too late. You can kill me if you like, but please leave Charlie. He's tried to undo Papa's mistakes and paid the price for it."

"*That means little to me. Why would I spare one of Papa's puppets? He is just as responsible for my fate as anyone else in this dying world, aside from Christopher.*"

"You don't understand, Ariane." The panic in her voice set in, but Matilda's temper rose regardless. "Do you know why he can't talk? Where he got those scars? He learned what our father really was, and Papa did *that* to him. By the time he recovered, you were already dead. Not everyone knew what Papa was planning. Not until it was too late to act. Some of us wanted to help."

The big man coughed and rolled over, clutching his stomach. The dead corpses that attacked him had clearly left their mark all over his beaten body. Charlie looked up at Archer with slit eyes.

"*What do you care about a mere goon, Matilda? He's no man of class like you always told me you wanted. You always said you deserved better. That is why you never left Papa, isn't it? You were afraid of poverty or being seen as lesser than your station. Who is this man to you?*"

"He found me sitting alone in the garden after you ran away from home. I deliberately separated myself from everyone, but Charlie went out of his way to talk. He taught me about azaleas and the right way to take care of the rose bushes Mama planted when we were younger. The two of us hit it off. He gave me a ring a week before Papa brought you back from the hospital. Papa didn't react well to the news—Charlie was just hired muscle to him. We were going to leave here and run away, just like you did, but now it's too late. Just please, don't kill Charlie. He's all I have left."

"*Run them both through, Christopher. Give me their hearts!*"

That familiar warmth pumped into Archer's heart. It was time for blood.

"No, don't!" Matilda shouted.

Archer let out a relieved breath. Now he could finally gather more gore for the spear and that searing sensation in his soul could be quenched. More flesh, more pain!

He no longer remembered why he was there on the moon. The constant screaming of the dead in his soul and the overwhelming flame in his fire-scorched gut just needed to be satiated and fed. The prey cowered right there in front of him, begging to be consumed. He salivated just thinking about the meal he would have.

Archer brandished his spear and stomped towards the couple. Dust plumed from his heavy steps. Two sacks of meat! He wouldn't just get one bite, but a full course meal. That familiar ecstasy doused his brain with pleasure. Saliva dribbled down his blackened lips.

"Christopher!" Matilda shouted. Her breaths stiffened the closer he approached. "Please! You must stop! Why would you kill Charlie? He was always on your side."

None of that nonsense mattered anymore. Archer's thoughts hollowed to nothing but a desire for pleasure. Blood was ahead—and blood was all that mattered.

"*Kill them, Christopher!*"

He gazed down at the trembling Matilda. Devouring her would have been so easy, but the look on her face made him want to do it now. Blood always tasted better when wrapped in misery. She leaped up and pushed him. He didn't budge, but she stood tall, outstretching her arms before Archer in protection of Charlie. The spear-wielder smiled at her feeble effort. All this free blood was like a gift from the heavens.

Heavy breathing replaced any speech Archer was capable of. Nothing that this husk of a woman said mattered regardless of what she squawked. Blood was meant for drinking, and nothing else.

Matilda's hard stare betrayed the tears in her eyes. "I already said you can have me—not him."

Archer lifted the spear, and she dropped to her knees. Her eyes closed, and he felt a small tremor in the back of his mind. It pried at his clenched muscles.

"*Don't listen, Christopher. Impale that wench! Give me her heart!*"

There were thoughts he had forgotten, feelings that had overtaken all the logic hiding in the back of his brain. An outside force scrubbed at his mind, trying to erase his thoughts and memories. The grip on his spear wavered as he attempted to remember what he thought he should. Shattered bits of memories burst in his mind, allowing him to remember the girl cowering at his feet.

Matilda McKinney, the woman who had helped him to escape from her father. But why was she on her knees with her arms out? She shouldn't be scared of him. Archer's head fuzzed, and the thought of delicious blood drilled into his soul. He bit his lip and shut his eyes—why couldn't he think properly?

"*Scorch her to ash!*"

Archer's body jerked as his eyes opened. The girl would

die. He brought the spear down onto the delicious flesh.

The weapon plunged downwards, piercing skin. Green blood oozed out of the wound. Archer had to blink a few times to realize what had just happened. Did he do that?

More surprising was that the flesh he cut into wasn't that of Matilda McKinney. Standing between himself and the girl was Charlie, his palm pierced by the spear. The neon blood leaked down the back of his hand as he wavered and quivered. The spear had been run through his hand. The big man grimaced and held the weapon still.

"Get off!" Archer said, with a surprising roar. "The dead have no rights."

Matilda shot up behind Charlie. "What are you doing? He's going to kill you!"

Charlie glistened with sweat, and his blood-caked skin paled even further, but still he would not relinquish the spear. It trickled sparks of fire along has hand. Matilda pulled at his waist.

"Get away, Charlie!" she said. "Listen to me for once!"

But Charlie held fast to the spear with his non-injured hand as cascades of flame rippled into his flesh. He looked into Archer's eyes without a hint of the coldness he usually held. The big man watched his aggressor with a pleading stare, as if to ward him off. Odd memories and pictures flowed into Archer's mind while he attempted to understand this wretch.

The girl screaming behind the fool and the shouting inside Archer's head merged into a thunderous symphony roaring out of tune. He clenched his teeth at the pins boring into his mind.

Moments of Charlie with his dead friend Miles and his girl Matilda slipped into Archer's thoughts. They collided with the memories of Ariane and the blood ache he had grown to love so much, spinning into a tornado of pulsating emotions.

A different kind of burning raged inside Archer's soul, knocking against the spear he held so tight and causing his grip to waver.

Faces merged and separated in his head as if puzzle pieces had been forced apart and the wrong parts had been smashed in place of the correct ones. Nothing made sense, but now he saw it for what it was. A foreign agent wanted to control him—it wanted them all.

Archer roared, and the flames leaped out of the spear. He kicked with a righteous fury, striking Charlie's abdomen. The giant doubled over, spitting saliva all over, as the weapon dislodged from his palm. Archer backhanded him down to the dirt, panting wildly. Matilda ran to her man's side as Archer desperately tried to regain balance. Blood rushed inside his skull. Who were these people again?

"*Why don't you kill him?*"

Archer winced. Actual red blood dripped like tears from his eyes. Had something changed inside of him? "What has he done to me?"

"*They all took you from me. We can never be together again, because of them.*"

"No, that's wrong. They are—I remember them."

Matilda wrapped Charlie's wounded hand with a piece of her dress while taking a glance back at Archer. She looked at him like he was a wild beast that could bite at any moment. But he wouldn't attack. They weren't trying to kill him. The overwhelming heat that had filled his being dulled, leaving only numbness in its place. Despite his lack of feeling, red blood seeped from his pores, ears, and mouth. The spear wanted more life-force, and he was running low on what he had to offer. If he didn't kill them now, the spear would eat him next.

"*You will die, Christopher! You have to devour them.*"

"There's only one man I have to kill." Archer stared

down at the couple watching him intently. "I don't know what will happen when I kill your father, so I'll just apologize now. It will never happen again. Watch your woman, Charlie. Do what I couldn't."

Matilda looked at Archer askew. "You're you again? But wait a second. What are you going to do?"

"I'm going into the sun."

"You can't just jump into the Eye from here. It's impossible."

"That's not actually the sun, and we're not in outer space. Your father created this universe through his summonings, but he can't touch me as long as I hold this spear. It's the only thing that can rip the fabric of this place apart. We're outside of time and space, so when he goes, it all goes."

"What about Ariane? What will happen to her?"

"That's my problem. Stick with Charlie, girl. He really has a thing for you. He was looking for towns to run to a month ago."

Charlie's eyes widened, and Matilda looked back and forth between them. She gaped. "How did you know what he was doing that long ago?"

"I saw it. Every time I cut someone, I see the life I'm taking. People and places far beyond me, whole other lives that are playing out without my input. I'm just one piece on the board, and I'm the only one here who can move in for checkmate. So that's what I'm going to do."

Archer crouched, felt the fire flow through his legs, and leaped. His jump launched him off of the moon and out through space. Without the dead of space to hold him back, he bolted like a rifle shot. Archer blitzed through the false universe towards the flaming Eye of the sun without anything to stop him. Hundreds of millions of miles passed like nothing in this constructed universe, unable to do anything to stop his approach.

A trickle of cold fear ran through him when he re-membered what fate awaited him in the death orb ahead. In that mass of memories from Charlie, Archer had regained his own self, and the knowledge of how much time he had left. His entire skin under his clothes had turned charcoal black, sizzling. He could no longer feel any part of his body. There was no coming out of this for Christopher Archer.

"Watch close, Ariane. I'll take you home myself. Just wait for me."

Chapter XI
Beyond the Sun

"You've found me!"

Those words reverberated in Archer's head from the night he ended up here. The road filled with red fog, and his headlights refused to pierce the blanketed pavement ahead. Before he could decide to pull over, she appeared before him in the center of the street. She warned him to turn back, but it was too late for Archer. Ariane had spoken to him again for the first time in months, and the joy so overwhelmed him that he didn't notice the car overturning until it was too late.

Now, as he soared through the universe of illusion before him, he remembered those old dreams. Ariane had been crying out to him since she was kidnapped, and yet he didn't know it. No wonder she had allowed herself to fall into despair. It was all his fault.

Ariane's voice booming in his ears died out as Archer focused on his forward trajectory through space. His body fired like a cannonball, streaking across the dead void of the artificial universe. The false stars twinkled and died the closer he reached the Eye in the center of this makeshift galaxy. If he could still feel anything, he might have allowed for joy to break through, but his numbed insides forbade everything. Only his drive kept him moving while the rest of him died.

The flames around the impossible sun blinked, the pupil dilated, and the fire around it blackened and burst outwards in impossibly long vine-like streams of harsh light.

Voices bounced around the inside of Archer's head. They screamed nonsense and bloody murder along with their empty threats. But one voice floated above the din.

"*Are you here to return my spear?*"

Red blood ejected out of Archer's mouth. "I'm going to shove it through your heart, McKinney."

"*You still don't understand, rodent. This is my universe.*"

Sparks split from the red sun, blinding Archer. A strange white light momentarily overtook his senses and broke the glint of the impossible sphere. The closer he approached, the more it became clear that it wasn't what it seemed at first. He saw inside the Eye's illusion to its true self.

A tall and fat organ not unlike a heart showed itself. It ran seven hundred thousand kilometers in radius with over a million in diameter. The circumference ran four million kilometers and the heart pumped inside the enormously impossible sphere, highlighted by purple mist in the empty void of space surrounding it. Above the heart swirled a cyclone of small ephemeral bird-like black outlines that looked something like people. He recognized hundreds of thousands of these ghosts of men, unmoving as if they were dead insects caught in a sink drain. The red tendrils fastened these lost souls to the pumping heart, as if they were hundreds of aortas, atriums, or pulmonary arteries, connected to an invisible source. This obscene organ was using these souls to siphon something, either from them or *through* them.

Archer had met the true form of the Eye: a parasite reshaped in the image its bearer had made for it. He didn't understand how he knew this, aside from the voice in his head whispering random knowledge he should not know. It could only be his weapon. The spear knew more than it let on. It wanted Archer to drain those souls for itself.

But Archer didn't fret. Any sense of fear he might have had died off with the rest of him. Ash sprayed through his tattered clothes, and he felt much lighter. His body had begun to crumble, and soon there would be nothing left of Christopher Archer but a memory. Nonetheless, he soared onward.

"*Even if you do run me through, you will still die. I see all, Archer. The spear has abandoned you.*"

"The spear doesn't matter, McKinney. You'll see. Just wait for me."

"*This will not do you any good!*" The fear in that ephemeral voice was palpable. McKinney's panicked tone brought some semblance of joy to Archer's dead heart. "*Stop!*"

Archer felt nothing below his waist. His legs had evaporated to nothing. The skin on his arms no longer existed, only charred muscles and bones remained to glisten in the crimson starlight. But a force beyond him kept Christopher Archer's insides together as he burst into the gigantic heart's airspace.

"*I will give you immortality! Just like the others. You can be with Ariane, Christopher! Just stop and you can have anything you want. Just stop!*"

"Don't chicken out now—it'll be over soon."

"*Wait!*"

The disintegrating man plunged onward. A thousand yards, one hundred yards, fifty yards, forty yards, twenty-five yards, he fired toward the center of the sun-sized titanic heart. His chest crumbled into the void, but he didn't even feel it. He didn't need to feel anything anymore.

The yelling in Archer's ear from countless suffering souls almost deafened him, but he could only think about *her.*

Ariane was waiting for him, and he promised to take her back home.

Gusts of barely visible needle-like pins plunged through Archer like scorpion tails. Red blood pooled on his lips, and his remaining muscles caught in a spasm. And yet he didn't stop his forward momentum. This enemy force wouldn't be enough. The needle stabs passed through him like a bad cold. McKinney could no longer stop his trajectory.

Archer crashed into the giant heart, ripping into the soft rippling surface with the spear. A beast-like howl caught in a hurricane swirled out into the abyss of space. Archer rocketed forward with his speed and burst through the flesh-covered tissue of the organ. Wind whistled behind him as chunks of the makeshift heart and tar-like blood flew back out into the abyss.

Pinkish and red vibrating ceilings and walls adorned the insides, but the path forward was otherwise empty aside from the flapping viscera. The yowling continued unabated as he soared toward the center of the impossibly massive, split-open organ.

A naked old man awaited in the center of the heart, his legs grafted into the piled up pink floor, and his arms melted into the similarly gruesome ceiling. Flesh tendrils rolled up into the pumping ventricles that climbed the millions of kilometers of this interior. A loud hiss cried out inside like a split steam pipe as Archer tore through it all.

McKinney shouted at Archer's approach. *"You're killing us all!"*

"We're all already dead."

"With both the Eye and the spear, we could change everything. No more death, no one being taken away from you, or me. You're throwing away our sacrifices!"

"This spear was made to kill the Eye, McKinney. It was made for this moment. All your scheming and struggling has only delayed the inevitable. This was always going to happen. Don't hate anyone but yourself for what's about to happen."

"You bastard! You stole everything from me, and you have the nerve to take more? You're nothing, rodent."

"And now, so are you."

Archer shot forward and drove the spear deep into McKinney's chest, through his heart. The old man bellowed, and wildfire dumped out of the weapon, consuming him as if he were already doused in gasoline. The flames slowly swirled into his body before shooting outwards and burrowing into the surrounding flesh of the inhuman heart. McKinney's skin, bones, and organs, scorched away into nothing but atoms as his bloodcurdling screams echoed into the depths of this false space.

Instantly, the quaking returned, as did the burning blood in Archer's remaining bones. Uselessly, he floated forward and out of the heart and back into space, his skin incinerated and tore itself apart. His vision faded as his eyes crumbled. Above his reeling remains, space itself split open, and the gigantic heart broke apart into the void from the tornado of flames until it too became nothing but ash. Death had consumed this entire universe.

And it was doing the same to him.

"What is this?"

Red-colored joy flooded his dead corpse of a body. His sight returned, as did his missing limbs and organs, reforming as if the universe had decided to rewind reality for him. His skin kept its blackened tone, as it always would from the spear, but McKinney's blood had given Christopher Archer new life.

The hunger returned, fiercer than it had ever been, but now he was alone. The Eye shrieked inside the spear, pleading for mercy as it frantically pointed the way out of this hell. Archer could tear apart the very fabric of space itself, and this madness would finally end. He could easily do it. With the Eye at his side, he had more power than a god.

Archer twisted, slashing open space itself, and the stars screamed like the souls of the damned. Outer space split, and the dark blue skies of midnight showed itself in the fissure. Earth was just ahead of him. The false universe shattered and cracked like a vandalized window around this new opening. Soon, this entire place would be nothing but a memory, and he would be free to roam Earth.

"No," he said. The spear beckoned him to go forth. "Not yet."

"*Stop!*" Ariane yelled into his ears. "*This is enough. Wake up, Christopher!*"

He grinned through his blood-stained lips. "So you are still there."

"*No, I—*"

"It's okay. The spear isn't going to win. There is only way to stop this thing's cycle, because there's only one way to deny it what it wants. Without a host, it is useless."

"*Don't!*"

"Even if I get back to Earth, this hunger will control me until I die. Sorry, Ariane. It's got to be my way."

"*Christopher . . .*"

Archer turned the spear on himself and ran it through his own heart. A thousand souls screamed at once inside his brain. Flames traveled up through his skull with excruciating agony, before it also consumed his flesh and existence whole.

The last thing he saw was the artificial universe around him breaking away to nothing, stars splitting and planets fading to dust as reality overtook this false place. Countless screams in his soul extinguished to nothing in the dark, as the cold grip of death consumed them all. Eventually, he died with them. Finally, reality resumed its normal course.

The dream had finally ended.

CHAPTER XII
Found

Betty-Ann watched him pack the last of his things into the car. He admired her spirit and energy, being up so early in the morning, and yet she had to know why he was leaving. She tried to tell Christopher Archer to stay, but she knew it was a losing game.

As he pulled out of the lot, he looked at the apartment building one last time. Those old rusty balconies and sliding doors that stuck in the humidity had always annoyed him, but now he was beginning to have nostalgia for them. For the first time in his life, he felt an odd sadness about leaving home. Once more, he was moving on.

She leaned into his window, her brunette buns bumping into the ceiling. "Don't do anything, stupid, Christopher. She wouldn't want that."

"I know," he said. "Thanks for everything, Betty-Ann. Tell your husband to keep walking that mutt of his. It's getting fat."

"Good luck out there, Christopher. I mean it. It'll be better, one day."

He drove out into the road and left town behind forever. He traveled for what could have been an eternity, though he didn't keep track. The wanderer stopped at motels, and the cold sweat waking him in the middle of the night. The whispers of a woman he loved more than he knew how to. He had that Beretta to keep him company, but it never spoke back— not like she did. The stark skies darkened in what felt like an eternal sunset the further he drove on as the days went on. This emptiness would never end, he just knew it.

But then the red mist swam over the road and enveloped him. In that dark night, he saw the lone figure emerge out of the woods. Her golden red hair fell over her pale face. A ghost, a specter of a dead past, approached him, begging for death. She had been waiting for him to put her out her misery. She was—

"*No!*"

His eyes opened in a flash.

Hard heat, burning like a fireplace, kindled somewhere nearby. It crackled in his ear. Warmth brushed Christopher Archer's cheek as a feather duster would. The sensation rubbed harder and harder with each stroke upon his skin. The grating continued before shot waves of pain shot through him. The razorblade-like blaze awakened his brain.

But there wasn't much to be awakened for. The stink of charred flesh choked the breaths he tried to take in, and the barren cave floor held a thin slime-like substance that reminded him of congealing blood. The heavy muggy heat pushed down on his bare shoulders and caused sweat to pour down his naked frame.

Where did his clothes go? Christopher patted himself down and discovered not only were his clothes gone, but so were his wounds. His skin was no longer scorched black, but the usual pinkish Caucasian tint again. None of these discoveries stopped the constant pain from transmitting through his bones. He found standing difficult with muscles jerking and struggling to support his weight. No light brightened this cavern, but he could see through it—as if his eyes had always been used to this darkness.

Shattered bits of metal and a crumbled thin shaft lay on the ground: the remains of the spear. It no longer gave out any signs of life of spoke to him. He would have confused it for scrap if the busted base wasn't so ingrained in his mind. A thin trail of black smoke wafting from it: the spear was evaporating.

He ignored the dead parasite and left the broken weapon behind to rot in the dark.

His unsteady steps carried him into a series of stone tunnels that winded onward up, down, left, and right, in countless directions. But there was only one road forward—the one that called him onward. There were no other paths or places to get lost in since they were the wrong way, whatever that way was supposed to lead to. He just seemed to know the right direction. That didn't prevent the confusion of his current state from hitting him. Where was he?

Despite the pitch black view, and the heavy heat, he couldn't detect a single other person nearby. McKinney was gone, as were Charlie and Matilda, and not even Doyle's annoying whine could be heard. No voices, no breaths, and not even a distant clatter. That was fine with him. All that mattered now was *her*. He had gotten accustomed to her voice, as corrupted as it was by the flames of the spear, but he couldn't go without the sound of Ariane's soft tones anymore. He knew who she really was, underneath it all. The silence of the tunnels caused chills to dance along his bare back. What if he never saw her again? That wasn't a possibility he could accept.

The stink of burnt flesh tickled his sinuses. His head pounded. Muscles and bones wanted to crumble from fatigue, even though he had no visible wounds. None of this made sense. Was he dead? Where exactly was he and what held him together?

A woman lay naked in the center of the path. Her golden red hair and pale, unblemished skin were unmistakable. Christopher ran towards Ariane, tripping over his own feet and falling all over himself to reach his fiancé. Stars crossed his vision mixed with the throbbing in his skull. Nonetheless, it didn't compare to the weight lifting from his heart and lungs after just seeing her the once.

He cradled Ariane in his arms. Her smaller, softer body slept silently against his chest. He took her forward through the cave, even though his bones now pained him twice as much as they did before. They didn't want him to bring her along. By all accounts, he should leave her, after all she had done. Too bad that his body had no say in what he was going to do.

"Christopher," she whispered. Her eyes were watery, blurry slits. "Do you hate me?"

"I know what it's like being under the control of emotions you can't contain. You would never make me kill, if you could help it. I don't blame you."

"The spear had so much . . . *bloodlust*. I didn't disagree with it. I really did want them all to die. I wanted to grind their corpses into the dirt, especially after everything they did."

"Mission accomplished. Do you want a medal? Whatever you're guilty of, I am twice as complicit. The only difference is that I willingly pulled the trigger. Not you. I'm willing to deal with the consequences, if we ever get out of here."

"I'm sorry," Ariane said. She took a hard breath. "Just leave me here. I don't deserve your help."

"Unfortunately, that's not up to you. You didn't have to approach me in that library back home. You didn't have to stand by me when I had no one. Did you think I wouldn't do the same? I came to this place for you, Ariane. I can't hate you. I bore the same rage you did. I'm willing to pay the price for it, with you."

"Are we still in the spear? I don't feel the heat, or any of the others. Do you think Matilda and Charlie are okay? They were the only ones still alive. I never even got to tell her I was sorry."

"Matilda's a smart girl. I'm sure she understood, especially after I left them behind. I'm gonna have to buy Charlie a drink to make up for what I almost did. But as for where we are? It doesn't matter, the spear is gone. There's only one way forward, so we're going to take it."

"I don't know if you, or anyone else, should forgive me. I dragged you into this, and I pushed you to do horrible things, for my sake. I couldn't escape Papa's hold, even though I ran so far away. He made me lose everything."

"What's done is over, Ariane. But what matters is where we're going. We can go anywhere now. Where do you want to spend the honeymoon?"

She forced a smile, and, even in his wincing state, his heart couldn't help but mindlessly hop inside of his heavy chest. It had been so long. "I'll go wherever you go, Christopher."

Ariane soon slipped back into slumber. Her breaths fell light again as her head rolled into his chest. He fought the urge to watch her at peace and kept his eyes on the winding path ahead of them. All that rage and hate had drained her. She had left it behind, and put her trust in him now.

Though he continued onward, it did not appear as if much progress was being made. Charred bones and blackened rocks were all he met along the way. His steps were the only sound he heard, and he still didn't know how he could see so well without any light source down in the dark.

An awkward sensation pressed heat against his sore muscles. A sudden, stabbing cold wind snapped through him so fast he couldn't be sure it was real. The weather was unstable in this place, and it didn't look to settle any time soon. But that was all the motivation he needed to keep moving through this never-ending cold and heat and the blanket of darkness. The bloodlust had departed entirely, allowing his weary mind to think again. Now he could focus on what truly mattered.

The nightmare was nearly over, and soon they could both finally awaken from this slumber. The day they could both look upon the real sun again would arrive, and they would meet it together.

Someday.

Local Community Report

On July 13th, 20XX, at approximately 3:45am, two suspicious persons spotted near the northern woods by Miller Way and Dyson.

A resident couple living on Carson Road were awoken by a knock on the door from a man and a woman wearing dirty, torn clothes. One of the individuals, a large man with a scarred lip, refused to speak. The second, a young woman with red hair, calmly and politely requested directions to the nearest bus station. The unknown couple disappeared down the road after obtaining the desired information. Witness speculation is that the suspects boarded the first morning bus at 5am.

No further disturbances reported.

About the Author

JD Cowan is a writer with an obsession for stories and Truth. He takes pleasure in looking for Light in the places where darkness grips the tightest. His works include "Someone is Aiming for You & Other Adventures", "Gemini Warrior" for Silver Empire, and short stories in Storyhack, the PulpRev Sampler, and the Planetary Anthology Series. His works can found at Amazon.

He blogs at wastelandandsky.blogspot.ca and can be found on Twitter @wastelandJD for those interested.

JD's Works

Knights of the End
Grey Cat Blues
Someone is Aiming for You & Other Adventures
Brutal Dreams
The Pulp Mindset: A NewPub Survival Guide

Gemini Man Series

Gemini Warrior
Gemini Drifter
Gemini Outsider [*Coming Soon!*]

www.ingramcontent.com/pod-product-compliance
Lightning Source LLC
Chambersburg PA
CBHW030305130626
46549CB00002B/704